CLAY RANDALL

SIX-GUN BOSS

Complete and Unabridged

LINFORD
Leicester

First published in the United States by
Random House

First Linford Edition
published 2021
by arrangement with
Golden West Literary Agency

A catalogue record for this book is available
from the British Library.

ISBN 978–1–78541–960–7

Published by
Ulverscroft Limited
Anstey, Leicestershire

Printed and bound in Great Britain by
TJ Books Ltd., Padstow, Cornwall

This book is printed on acid-free paper

SIX-GUN BOSS

The three big cattle outfits of New Orlando are being bled dry by rustlers. Pat Reagan, range detective for the Texas Panhandle Stockmen's Association, is assigned to work undercover as a ranch hand for George Albert of the Box-A, and bring the thieves to justice. But the only law around there is that of the six-gun and the noose — and when the glamorous daughter of George makes a play for Pat, he's heading into deep trouble . . .

This Book Is For Gerry

1

The whole thing got started with a letter. I was up in the Panhandle at the time, where the Association had sent me to help the ranchers clear up an epidemic of brand splotching. But that job was over.

Somehow, the road agents in the badlands let a stage get through from Fort Worth, and that was how the letter got to me. It was short and to the point, as John Barlow's letters always were. 'Got a job for you,' it said. 'Place called New Orlando. Rustlers, bushwhackers, range wars. Drop whatever you're doing and get to it.'

I wasn't doing anything in particular, except spending my hard-earned money on bad whiskey and shady women in Panhandle saloons. The letter was signed 'John Barlow, President, Texas Cattlemen's Association,' and there was a P.S. that added: 'See man named George

1

Albert, Association member.'

I didn't know where New Orlando was, but I went down to the livery barn and talked to the stableman, and found out that it was in the western part of the state somewhere, south of Salt Fork but not as far as the Pecos.

★ ★ ★

It turned out to be a long ride from the Panhandle to New Orlando. It's desert most of the way, greasewood and sage and not much else in the way of scenery. About the fourth day out you catch yourself talking to the prairie dogs just to hear a human voice again.

And they've got a sun in that part of Texas that is the grandfather of all suns. About six in the morning it comes up big and red and lazy-looking and you think it's going to be a nice day; then about five minutes later it explodes like a warehouse full of blasting powder. You begin reaching for your canteen, and if your canteen's empty you start looking

2

around for a barrel-head cactus to cut up to squeeze a few drops of juice on a tongue that is getting too big for your mouth. About the sixth day you begin to decide that you didn't want to go to New Orlando anyway.

But if you're a stock detective you'll probably keep plodding along, because you won't have any better sense. In that case — if your horse and the barrel-head cactus hold out — you'll finally get to New Orlando.

I got my first look at the place late one afternoon, after the sun had decided that it had dehydrated everything in sight for that day and was lazing along the western edge of the badlands.

I almost turned around and went back. I didn't have to be a stock detective. I could homestead a place somewhere and build a squatter's nest, and wear bib overalls and brogans, and ride work mules the rest of my life. I could, but I didn't think I would like it. Not even the two gents decorating the cottonwood could convince me that I'd like it.

The cottonwood was on a little knoll of high ground about a mile from town. New Orlando set down at the bottom of the grade near a small river, or creek, a flea-bitten little false-fronted town looking fagged and wrung-out at the end of the hot day. That cottonwood was the thing that caught my interest, though.

I couldn't tell just how long they had been up there, but it couldn't have been more than a couple of hours. The buzzards hadn't got to them yet.

There were two of them. They had ropes around their necks and their eyes popped out like squeezed grapes. They swung to and fro in a slight breeze, about four feet off the ground. Their faces were black and bloated all out of shape, like the faces you see on bodies that have been in water too long. They could have been my brothers and I wouldn't have recognized them.

'Well, boy,' I said, 'it looks like justice has gone off on another spree. Maybe our job has already been taken care of. Would you say these two gents look like rustlers?'

I was talking to that yellow horse of mine, a habit that most cowhands fall into sooner or later.

Somehow, it didn't seem right to leave the two bodies hanging up there for buzzard bait, so I nudged Dusty over and cut them down. I didn't have anything to bury them with, but maybe somebody in town would take care of that, when they got around to it.

It was just beginning to get dark when I rode into the town. There was that uneasy, on-edge feeling in the air that comes at the end of a trying day. Supper's late, the kids cry. Everything is going wrong, and chances are that it will get worse before it gets better. What I needed was a drink.

But I took Dusty down to the livery barn first, where an ancient stableman with a bottle breath agreed to take care of him. I washed up at the livery pump and beat some trail dust out of my clothes. When I went back into the barn the old man was hanging on the feedbag.

'Give him all the corn he wants,' I said.

He grunted, telling me that he was taking care of horses before I was out of square pants.

'I guess you must have had some excitement in town today,' I said.

No answer.

'About a mile back I noticed a couple of citizens decorating a cottonwood.'

He slapped my horse on the rump and said, 'All right, Buck, let's get in the stall.'

'Maybe it's something you don't want to talk about,' I tried.

He slammed the gate to the stall. I gave up. I went out to find the nearest saloon.

There was a place about four doors down called the Star Bar, a run-of-the-mine place, no sawdust on the floor, only two or three gambling tables in the rear, and no girls since this was the slack time of day. The bartender was lighting the hanging lanterns. There was a quiet party of three men at one of the tables.

I leaned on the bar and called to the bartender, 'I'll have some bourbon when you get around to it.' So he brought me a bottle and a tumbler.

'Slow,' he said.

I agreed that it was slow.

'New?' he asked.

I admitted that, too.

'Hot day,' he said. He wiped his face with a dirty bar apron.

I took another drink and decided that the citizens of New Orlando would never become noted for their loose talk among strangers. 'Look,' I said, 'I wonder if you'd tell me something?'

'That depends.'

'About an hour ago,' I said, 'I saw two men hanging from a cottonwood. They hadn't been there long, but they couldn't get any deader if they swung till the rope rotted. I'm just wondering what the trouble was.'

He looked at me and wiped his face again. He was a big lumpy man who couldn't take the heat as well as some. He didn't say anything. After a while I caught on that he wasn't going to say anything.

'Well,' I said, 'can you tell me where I could find a man named George Albert?'

He looked relieved, pointed at the table where the three men were sitting.

One of the men turned around when he heard his name mentioned. 'Are you looking for me, stranger?'

'If you're George Albert.'

'The only one in New Orlando,' he said.

'Well, I guess you're the man I want to see then.' I walked over and we shook hands. 'The name's Pat Reagan,' I said. 'You don't know me, but my boss in Fort Worth said if I was to come to New Orlando that maybe you'd give me a job.'

I didn't want to come right out and advertise the fact that I was a stock detective unless I had to. George Albert looked puzzled for a minute. Then it hit him. 'Well, I'll be damned,' he said. 'You got here in a hurry. I'll say that for you.'

I smiled, and the other two men at the table smiled back, without knowing why. 'Let me make you acquainted,' George Albert said. 'Pat Reagan, this here is

Kyle Northern, and the man over there is Ran Phillips.'

So I shook hands all around. Kyle Northern was a big blond man somewhere in his late thirties. Ran Phillips was the young rancher type, thin and thirty five and worried. The bartender brought a bottle over, but Northern and Phillips shook their heads and said it was getting to be their supper time.

'Join us?' Phillips said.

'I think I'll take some trail dust out of my throat first.' So they went out the door, Northern leaving some silver at the bar to pay for the drinks.

'Well,'. George Albert said, 'so you're a stock detective. I've often wondered what one of those things looked like.'

He was an easy-talking, gray-haired man in his middle fifties. His eyes were gray too, slightly faded from too much of this New Orlando sun. He wore a six-gun like everybody else, a fancy, silver-mounted job that would be fine to frame and hang over the fireplace, but not worth a damn for shooting. I figured that somebody had given it to him and he wore it just for the sake of appearances.

'This is quite a place to get to,' I said.

He nodded and smiled faintly. 'Yes, there's not much to the north of here except desert. More badlands to the west. But there's good grazing land to the south and east, along Hound Dog Creek. There's a dozen or so ranches around here. We sell our cattle over in New Mexico to the Indian reservations — when we've got any cattle to sell, that is.'

'Rustlers giving you trouble?' I asked.

He smiled that smile of his. 'Something's giving us trouble. Most of the small ranchers are on the ropes. Me and Northern and Phillips are the only ones with big spreads. We can absorb punishment better than the others, but pretty soon they're going to have us on our knees too.'

'Maybe you'd better start at the beginning and tell me about it.'

'Well,' he said, pouring from the bottle,' there isn't much to it. Like I said, the badlands are pretty close to here. They come from there, I guess, the rustlers. They hit fast, at nights mostly, cutting out anywhere from a dozen to a hundred head of cattle. Probably they take them across the border and sell them to some crooked Indian agent.'

I remembered something then. 'I've been trying to find out who strung up the crow bait north of town,' I said. 'Does that have anything to do with the rustling?'

George Albert shook his head sadly. 'So you saw that, did you? Well, it couldn't be helped. Kyle and Ran and myself, we tried to stop them, but the small ranchers are too riled up to be stopped. They were rustlers, all right, though. We caught them in a raid last night and put them in jail. We figured we could make them talk and then we'd know who was behind this thing.' He shrugged. 'But the ranchers got stirred up this afternoon and broke into the jail. You saw the rest of it.'

'Haven't you got any law in New Orlando?' I asked.

He spread his hands on the table. 'The Sheriff's just one man — a good man, too, but he couldn't do much with a mob like that.'

'Any idea who stirred them up?'

'No problem about that,' he said. 'One of the small ranchers, a newcomer here in New Orlando. Name of Kurt Basser.'

By that time the saloon was getting a few customers, most of them drifting in from an eating house across the street. After a while the saloon girls came in and began putting on their war paint for the evening trade.

I thought about what Albert had told me. If I was a man to jump at conclusions, the first jump I'd take would be at Kurt Basser. Lynching was a pretty handy way of shutting men up, although it probably wouldn't make him too popular with the rest of his employees. Assuming that Basser was the boss rustler, of course, which was pretty farfetched at this point.

I said, 'My boss said something about a range war. Does that tie up anywhere?'

George Albert looked surprised. 'Range war? Why there hasn't been . . . ' And then he laughed. 'Why, you must mean the little trouble with Ran Phillips a while back.'

'Maybe,' I agreed.

'Well, there wasn't anything to it. A little squabble over water rights. He's pretty hot-headed and is apt to fly off the handle once in a while. I knew his pa, and he was the same way. But it's all right now. You might say the rustlers pulled us together and made us see that we had to fight side by side.' I thought that over and couldn't make anything out of it. Then a girl came up to the table and I brushed her away.

'Not tonight, honey,' I said. 'I've just finished a long trip, and besides, I'm broke.'

George Albert's face turned brick red. Then he sat back with his mouth open and laughter rolled out of him. I felt my own face getting red then. My stomach curled up like a prodded armadillo and tried to hide behind my liver, which is the feeling I usually get when I know I've made a fool of myself. The girl was still standing there. Her face was drawn and white. It was a beautiful face, but now it was completely bloodless with rage.

I heard myself making apologies because I could see now that she was no saloon girl. I didn't know how I could have made the mistake in the first place.

By that time George Albert had had his fun, and he got up wiping his eyes with a pocket handkerchief. 'I should have warned you, Reagan,' he said between chuckles, 'that my wife sometimes has to come into the saloon to get me to go home.'

Then he was making the introductions. 'Marcia, this is Mr. Reagan. Mr. Reagan, my wife.'

I must have said something. I'm not sure. The wind had been pretty well knocked out of me — not so much because of the mistake I'd made, but because of Marcia Albert herself.

For one thing, she was young enough to be George Albert's daughter, twenty-five at the outside. Cut from the same cloth that real beauties come from. Dark hair framing an oval face, a mouth that was just right, eyes with fire in them. And the dress she wore hadn't been cut in New Orlando. Fort Worth, probably. It was filled out in just the right places, without benefit of padding.

Probably Mrs. Albert was used to being stared at. I looked at her hard enough to move a mountain, but after she got over her first spell of anger she didn't flinch.

Mr. Albert was getting his Stetson. 'Do you know where the Box-A is, Reagan? That's my outfit, you know.'

'I can find out,' I said.

'Do that. Come out tomorrow and we'll talk about that job of yours.'

Then we said good night all around. I smiled, and Mr. Albert smiled, and Marcia Albert smiled, and we were all friends again. Then they were gone.

I had another drink. I had two drinks. I counted my money and decided that was all I could afford. Then it hit me.

The idea had been moving around in

15

the bottom of my mind all the time, I guess, but now it popped to the top. I had seen Marcia Albert somewhere before. Where, I didn't know, but a woman like that you don't forget. But where had it been? I squandered another two bits and poured myself another drink. I still couldn't remember.

Well, I'd think of it sometime. I started to pour another drink and missed the glass. It was time to put some food on top of that whiskey.

I found the eating house across the street and had steak and eggs and potatoes, all served up together on a greasy platter. After eating, I left a silver dollar on the counter and went out on the plankwalk to pick my teeth and listen to the saloons getting tuned up for the night trade. It sounded like it was going to be a big night, and I was sorry I couldn't join in. Maybe another time, when I was rested up and had some silver to impress the girls with. I started down the street toward the livery stable to see if my close-mouthed friend would advance me sleeping room in his hayloft. I almost made it.

But not quite. I got as far as a feed store when a pair of hard cases with rock faces stepped out and began to take over.

'Well, well,' one of them said. 'A pilgrim. What's your name, pilgrim?'

The other one laughed. 'Maybe he ain't got a name, Huck. My, my,' he added sarcastically, 'he's carryin' a gun too. That shows he's tough.'

'He don't look so damn tough to me,' Huck said. 'How about it, pilgrim? Are you supposed to be tough?'

I kept walking. I've got a nose for trouble and I could smell it rolling in like a Panhandle sandstorm. It didn't work, though, trying to ignore it. The man called Huck grabbed my shoulder and jerked me around.

'What's the matter, pilgrim? A man asks a civil question, he expects a civil answer.'

Then I made a mistake. I said, 'Take your goddam hand off me!'

That's the trouble with whiskey. Once it gets warm and comfortable in your stomach, it starts talking its head off. Huck blinked his eyes. For a minute I thought I was going to make the bluff stick. Then he grinned.

'Well, well,' he said. He was thinking about something that appealed to him very much. 'Well, well.' And about that time the other man caught me behind the ear with the barrel of a Colt's .45.

It's no fun to get hit like that by a man who means business. Pain knocks the top of your skull off and then shoots straight down to your groin, and then your insides turn to buttermilk and you start falling. If you have a particularly hard head or if you see the blow coming, maybe it won't knock you out. I had seen it coming, but not in time to do any good.

I fell to the plankwalk and hopped around. Just for fun, Huck took a couple of kicks at my ribs. The other one — a man called Kramer — had a turn. Finally, Huck jerked me up by the front of my shirt and I understood that the party was just getting started. They were experts. They had kicked just the right shoulder muscles to paralyze my arms for a while. They were having themselves a time, all right, and there was nothing I could do about it. It was a workmanlike job with not too much emotion mixed up in it. Kramer just kept things going until the other one got his brass knucks on. Finally he did get them on. I don't remember much after that.

At first I'd thought they were just a couple of cowhands full of redeye, out to work off a little steam. But it wasn't that at all. I caught on after a while.

They were out to kill me!

That was when my guts thawed out, I guess. I tried to fight back, but things were already too far along. I took a wallop from those brass knucks that crossed my eyes, that cut my mouth, that made my head ring.

My brains were all scrambled, but I was still trying to figure it out. Why did they want to kill me? Why didn't they shoot me?

I had the answer to that one. An uncalled-for shooting might cause trouble, even in New Orlando. But a common street brawl, that was something else. I was a stranger in town. I had been seen drinking — drinking heavy. All right, I got quarrelsome and picked a fight with two hard cases.

I could almost see them telling it to the Sheriff. Everybody would shake their heads sadly and they would crate me up in a pine box and haul me off to boot-hill, and that would be the last of old Pat Reagan. Not a tear shed. Not even a funeral, probably. I could hear the Sheriff telling them not to worry about it. It wasn't their fault. Damn strangers, any-way, trying to take over the town.

Something like that was the way my addled brain was working when the knucks connected for the second time. Then everything got very dark. I pitched head first into an ocean of black nothing-ness. George Albert, I thought, would have to catch the rustlers himself, or at least write another letter to the Associa-tion. The president wasn't going to like having one of his men killed either. He would have to start all over again and break in another one. The ocean got darker and darker and something kept bothering me as I went down. I'd never be able to remember where it was that I had seen Marcia Albert. I was sorry about that.

2

It was still dark when I came out of it. That was a surprise, because I hadn't expected to come out of it at all. But there I was, stretched out like a log on the hard, cold ground, too numb to know if I was going to live or die, and not caring much either way. My ribs were sore and it was hard to breathe. I had an idea that those ribs were going to be sore for a long time.

My arms seemed to end around the shoulders somewhere. That was because of the kicking they had taken. I was using a very fragile glass globe for a head. Empty, very delicate, made of the finest crystal. If I moved it would break. So I didn't move. I just lay there.

After a while I began to catch the moist, ammonia smell of horses and I figured I must be in a stable somewhere. How I got to a stable I couldn't guess. I lay quietly, breathing carefully, not disturbing that glass head of mine. Time passed. A minute or an hour. I thought about the big hombre called Huck, and the one only slightly smaller called Kramer. They had a nice down-to-earth way of working. Somebody had got himself a couple of good hands when he hired those two.

Not too dependable, though, I decided, after giving it some thought. They had started a job but they hadn't finished it. Wonder how come, though. They didn't just get tired and knock off the job. I knew them too well for that. Our acquaintance hadn't been a long one, but I knew them, all right. I wondered if I ought to try to get up. What would I do if I did get up? Nothing that I could think of.

Anyway, it was worth a try. I concentrated on moving my arms and discovered they would work, after a fashion. I got my elbows under me and shoved. Sweat broke out on my forehead and ran in my eyes. All right, Reagan, you're tough, a hundred and ninety pounds of bone and muscle. Let's get off the ground.

I couldn't do it. I could dogtrot from the Salt Fork to El Paso with a Napoleon cannon under each arm. I could swim the Rio Grande, carrying a gunny sack full of water-soaked buckshot. Those things were easy. But when it came to something really tough like getting my shoulders off the ground, I couldn't do it.

I must have dozed off then, because I didn't see the old man when he came.

It was my loose-talking friend, the stableman. He was no doctor, but he knew how to care for drunks who got themselves mangled in street brawls. There was a bucket of water in his hand. He sloshed it in my face like he was throwing slop to pigs.

That did it. It was the hard way, maybe, and not very gentle, but it brought me out of it. I sat up sputtering. The old man stared at me flatly.

After a while I found my tongue. It was a little hard to handle, but I still had it, and that was something. 'If there's any of that water left,' I said, 'just pour it in my mouth.'

He handed me the bucket and let me do my own pouring. I felt a little better. I said, 'The last I remember I was about a half a block down the street, going down for the third time. How did I get to your livery barn?'

He spat at the ground and wiped his mouth with the back of a scrawny hand. 'I toted you,' he said. 'Drug you, ruther. Too damn heavy to tote.'

'Did you stop the fight?'

He spat again, this time in the direction of a murderous-looking scatter gun leaning against a stable door. 'Whatever it was, I stopped it. Didn't look like much of a fight, though.'

'No, I guess it didn't. Well, thanks for sitting in and taking a hand.'

He didn't have anything to say to that. 'Did you see who they were?' I asked.

'Dark. Couldn't see much.'

'But you've got some ideas?'

I decided it was time to get up. I got on my hands and knees and lifted myself slowly, like a young ape just beginning to walk. It was hard work. I went over and sat on some hay.

'You got enemies,' the stableman said.

'It looks that way.'

'How come?'

'I don't know. I don't even know who they were. They called themselves Huck and Kramer.'

'Just names.'

He was a big help.

'Do you mind if I wash at your pump?'

'No.'

'I'd like to sleep up in your loft tonight, if that's all right with you. I expect to have a job tomorrow. I'll pay you for the space.'

'All right.'

I went outside and washed up. Maybe I was going to live, after all. I came back in and got a clean shirt out of my war bag. The old man was getting settled on a cot in the back of the barn. 'Well, thanks again,' I called. 'I hope I'll be able to pay you back someday.'

No comment.

I was too sore and tired to carry the conversation by myself. I went up to the loft and burrowed in the hay and let the darkness come.

★ ★ ★

I woke up the next morning into a world full of aches and pains. I had bruises and cuts that I hadn't even known about. Good old Huck and Kramer, whoever they were. I hoped we'd meet again sometime. I also hoped to meet the party that had them signed on his payroll. That was going to be a day to wait for. If I could manage to live that long.

The stableman was up and about and as talkative as ever when I came down from the loft.

'Leavin'?' he asked.

'I'm not going far, just out to George Albert's ranch. You know where that is?'

He got out about a quarter's worth of twist tobacco and gnawed on it. 'That would be the Box-A. Three, four mile southeast. Take the east road out of town. Don't mind the cut-off; that goes to Kyle Northern's place. You aimin' to

27

work for the Box-A?'

'Maybe.'

He went over and sat down on a block of salt. 'You want Buck saddled up?'

'The horse's name is Dusty. He won't answer to any other name,' I said. 'You can get him saddled while I go over and get some breakfast.'

As I walked off I heard him saying, 'Come on, Buck, let's get this rig on,' and that yellow horse was following him all over the barn.

* * *

The road out to George Albert's place was just a wagon track, like most of those roads are. But the farther south and east we got, the greener the grass got, and the more cattle we saw with big block A's on their hips, boxed in with a square. About half a mile in front of the ranch house we had to cross a cold little stream that I guessed was Hound Dog Creek. It came from the north and seemed to make a big bend to the south and then

28

head back toward New Orlando. It was pretty enough country. Or maybe it only seemed pretty because of the desert you had to cross to get there.

Anyway, the Albert ranch house was something to look at, no matter what the country was like. It was a squat, sprawling composition of adobe brick and rock and cottonwood logs, almost big enough to do the spring branding in. There were four chimneys on it, plenty of fireplaces so Marcia Albert wouldn't have to dress in the parlor on cold winter mornings.

I don't know why I kept thinking about her. It wasn't decent to keep thinking about men's wives. Not even for a stock detective. I tried to switch my mind onto something else — my aches and pains, this rustling business that the Fort Worth office was anxious about. It wasn't any good. Marcia Albert kept crowding into the picture.

There was a hitching rack in the front yard, so I left Dusty there and went up to the front door and knocked. I woke somebody. I heard quick steps in the dim interior. Then there she was.

Not Mrs. Albert. Somebody else. She was as pretty as Marcia, in a different kind of way, and about the same age. It was kind of a shock, two women like that in the same house. Maybe Albert collected wives the way some men collected old guns. If that was the case, he was off to a good start. Probably the best collection in Texas already.

'Yes?' she said.

It was just an ordinary voice, but there was something about it that hit you. She had blonde hair, done up the way women do it, at the nape of her neck. Her eyes were blue, I think, or gray. It was hard to tell.

I said, 'Ma'am, my name's Pat Reagan. I'd like to talk to George Albert, if he's somewhere around.' There was something about me that seemed to interest her. It was flattering until I realized that my face must look like hell. She didn't ask me to come in, and I couldn't exactly blame her. She started backing off and her voice got smaller and smaller.

'I'll see . . . Will you wait, please?'

I told her I'd be happy to wait, and I killed some time by rolling a cigarette and trying not to listen to a whispered powwow going on inside. Then Marcia Albert came to the door.

'I'm sorry,' she said, 'but Mr. Albert is awfully busy now. Could you come back tomorrow?'

'Another night like last night,' I said, 'and I wouldn't be able to make it tomorrow.'

Her eyebrows lifted, but that was all. She looked nice and fresh and clean, as if she had just been taken out of the crate.

'Well . . . very well. Please wait on the porch.' So I waited on the porch, me and a black horsefly breathing itself to death against the screen door. Maybe I should have shaved and shined my boots and pressed my pants before coming to call at the Box-A. Maybe I should have gone to the back door and talked to the chuck burner. I mashed my cigarette out on the clean porch, and after a while George Albert came to the door.

31

'Why, come in, Reagan. What are you doing out there?'

'It's this New Orlando air,' I said. 'I can't seem to get enough of it.'

'The air?' He didn't have his mind on it. But he pushed the screen open and let me in, and then he noticed my face. 'My God, what happened to you?'

'It's a long story,' I said. 'I'll get around to it after a while.'

We walked through the front room, the parlor I guess they called it. There was some good solid-looking oak furniture that looked like it might have come all the way from St. Louis. How they got it across the desert I don't know. There was a big braided rug on the floor that had kept half a dozen Mexican women busy for a year in the making; a fireplace big enough to barbecue an ox and over the fireplace a mounted buffalo head. A few antelope antlers were scattered around on the walls, along with a picture of an uncomfortable-looking gent about to choke to death in a Mexican War uniform, probably George Albert's old man.

We went down a hall and wound up in a leather-smelling room where one wall was covered with books, maybe six or seven hundred of them. Nobody in Texas did that much reading, not even George Albert. There was also a well-used, businesslike desk and a couple of cowhide-covered chairs in the room. Albert got behind the desk and I took one of the chairs and went to work on a cigarette.

'I used to have a place in the north wing of the house where I did the book work for the ranch,' Albert apologized, 'but Marcia — Mrs. Albert — wanted to make an extra bedroom out of it. Actually, though, this room is big enough for the work I do in it.'

I had seen families of nine living in rooms that were smaller, but I didn't bring that up. I said, 'Let's see if we can't drop a loop around a fact or two about this rustling business. First off, are you the only Association member here in New Orlando?'

33

'The only one I know of. That's the reason I didn't mention who you were yesterday. Ran Phillips' pa was dead against organizations of any kind, and I guess that's the reason Ran never joined up himself. Kyle Northern has been too busy, I guess. He started when he was just a bit of a kid with a little brush-popping outfit. Everything he got he had to work for.'

'Did you tell anybody that you were writing to the Association for help?'

'Why, no, I didn't tell a soul.'

'Not even your wife?'

'No, not even Marcia. Why do you ask?'

'Last night I ran into a pair of quick-draw artists. I think they had killing on the brain until something happened to stop them. I just wondered if somebody hadn't taken a sudden notion that they didn't want an Association man sticking his nose into things.'

George Albert frowned. 'Do you mean they tried to shoot you?'

'Gun barrels and brass knucks were

the tools they used. Do you know anybody who operates that way?'

'I can't remember the last time I saw a pair of knucks in Texas. What did they look like?'

I tried to remember. 'They were big men. Almost as big as I am. One of them had a beard, but not much of one. Dressed like anybody else. They called each other Huck and Kramer. It was pretty dark. I'd know them if I saw them, but I'm afraid I can't do much of a job describing them. I wish I'd seen them in daylight.'

Albert shook his head. 'I don't know. They could be almost anybody. Do you think they knew who you were?'

'Why else would anybody want to kill me?'

We thought about that one for a while.

'Well,' I said, 'let's get on with the rustling. Maybe you'd better just start at the beginning and tell me everything you can think of.'

He took a minute or two to get things organized. While he was doing it, he took a cigar from a leather covered box, bit off the end, wet it, lit it. 'Well,' he said, 'it hasn't been going on long. At first we thought it was just a raiding band up from Mexico making a pass through the country. But that wasn't it. When cattle kept disappearing it became clear that somebody was trying to clean us out — all the ranchers around New Orlando. That was when I wrote the Association.'

He puffed for a while to get his cigar to burn just right. 'I hate to say it,' he went on, 'but I'm afraid some of the ranchers themselves are behind it.'

'What makes you say that?'

'Well, for one thing, the rustlers know too much. They know just where our herds are, no matter how much we shift them around. They know where our line riders are, although we shift them too. And the extra riders, as well, that almost all the ranchers have hired in the past month or so. Then there's that lynching business that happened yesterday. If those men had lived to talk, maybe we would know who was the brains of the thing. But they didn't live.'

'You mentioned a man named Kurt Basser. What about him?'

'He drifted into town about two months ago. Just a tin-horn gambler, from the looks of him, but somehow he got enough money together to buy a little spread down to the south. He's a trouble-maker, but I don't think he's smart enough to be running a thing like this.'

'Well, let's see, what about the Indian agencies in New Mexico? Couldn't we get any help from them?'

'It's hard to get anybody to say any-thing when they're holding political jobs. Anyway,the Indian beef buyers are in it as deep as the rustlers, if that's where the cattle are going.'

'Then how about something direct and simple. What's wrong with organiz-ing a posse and going into the badlands after them?'

He looked at me pityingly. 'There are maybe three hundred square miles of badland — rock hills, caves, giant boulders, canyons. It would take a regi- ment of cavalry to Hush anybody out of country like that. No, the way I see it, our only chance is to catch them when they come down on the range, or catch the person behind it. We haven't been able to do either one.'

I sat there trying to look as if I had an idea. But I wasn't fooling anybody. After a while I said, 'I'd like to have some time to look things over. If you could put me up at the Box-A for a few days maybe I'll stumble onto something.'

'That won't be any trouble,' he said. 'I can put you on the payroll as a new rider. Everybody is hiring extra riders now.'

I said that would be fine, and speaking of payrolls . . . George Albert caught on. Maybe he was young and foolish himself once. He counted out forty dollars in gold and silver.

'The Association will make this good,' I said, 'when I get back to Fort Worth.'

The boss of the Box-A wasn't interested in forty dollars. What he wanted was his cattle back.

I had intended to set up housekeeping

in the regular bunkhouse, but Albert said there was plenty room where the foreman lived and I could stay there. We turned Dusty over to the wrangler and threw my war bag on the floor and I was moved in.

It was quite a place, considering it was just the foreman's house. A log affair complete with kitchen, front room and a couple of sleeping rooms. It had its own dog-trot and a private outhouse. Nothing fancy, but plenty good enough for the likes of a ranch foreman.

'It used to be a family place,' Albert said. 'We had a foreman with a wife and two boys a few years back. But the wife got homesick for Kansas, so they moved. Vic Schuyler is our foreman now. He rode out to one of the line camps, I think, but you'll see him around sundown.'

Albert went back to the ranch house. I picked out the room that seemed to have the softest bunk and stretched out, trying to figure out a way to give my new boss his forty dollars' worth. While I was working on it I went to sleep.

I woke up in the shade of a big red-faced giant leaning against the door frame, grinning at me. He was at least six-four. Two hundred and ten pounds. Maybe two-twenty. No fat at all.

'Howdy!' he said.

The voice came from about twelve miles down, big and rich. I got my boots off the bunk. Maybe it was *his* bunk.

'Howdy,' I said. 'You must be Vic Schuyler. I'm Pat Reagan.'

I got up and we shook hands. 'The boss told me you was here,' he said loudly. 'Glad to have you. Like company once in a while. House like this gets lonesome, just one person all the time.'

I was glad he felt that way about it, considering the size of him.

'Did Mr. Albert tell you anything else?' I asked. 'Just that you was a new hand he'd hired on. I figured there's somethin' funny, though. He never bunked just a rider with me before.' He ducked his head and went through the doorway into the kitchen. He came back with a two-gallon vinegar jug with something in it that didn't look like vinegar, and two tin cups. He poured the cups brim full and handed me one.

'By God,' Vic Schuyler said, 'a man needs a drink of something after ridin' all day in that sun.' And with that he turned the cup up and drained it. I don't suppose it ever occurred to him that water was pretty good at quenching a man's thirst. I had a go at my cup.

'It don't make any difference to me, though,' Vic said, wiping his mouth with the back of a hairy hand. 'Whatever the boss says is all right. Just kind of make yourself at home around here. What do you think about that whiskey?'

'It's whiskey, all right.'

'Rye,' he said. 'Here, let me fill her up. Get it from a nester I know, makes it himself. I don't like this goddam cornslop you get in saloons. Hogs get better than that up in Dakota.'

'Is that where you're from, Dakota?'

'Sure. Coldest damn place in the world in the winter. No place for raisin' cattle; that's the reason I come to Texas.'

He filled my cup to the brim again, pulled up a cane-bottomed chair and sat down, very carefully. He had probably broken a lot of chairs in his time. We sat there looking at each other. Here, I thought, is a man I want on my side.

'Look,' I said, 'I think I'd better show my hand.' He shrugged. 'All right. But like I said, it don't make a damn to me.' Then he grinned. 'What are you, a stock detective?'

'How the hell did you know that?'

'Didn't know it. Just guessed. It all ties in, though — rustler trouble, a strange rider comes in and bunks with the foreman. And the boss belongs to the Association; I knew that.'

'Well,' I said, 'I guess I don't have to tell you anything, after all.'

We drained the cups again. After that somebody rang a dinner gong and we made our way to the cook shack.

* * *

That night I found out who the second woman was in George Albert's house. Vic Schuyler was bumping around the kitchen in his long red underwear, pouring himself another cup of rye before going to bed. 'Got in the habit of wearin' them the year round up in Dakota,' he called. 'Feel naked without them. What was that you said?'

'I said who's the blonde-haired girl over in the ranch house?'

'The old man's girl. Daughter, that is. She wasn't here when I started work three years ago. Down in Mississippi somewhere, goin' to some fancy school. She come back a while after the boss got married. Name's Jane.'

'Well, George Albert keeps a fine collection of women around. I'll say that for him.'

No comment from the kitchen.

'Say, where did Mrs. Albert come from anyway?' Vic Schuyler appeared in the doorway, one ham-sized hand swallowing a tin cup.

'Why?'

'No reason in particular. I've just got a feeling that I've seen her somewhere.'

I thought the foreman's eyes narrowed just a little. 'You never seen her,' he said. 'Mrs. Albert came from back East. The boss married her when he was back there on a buying trip. She's a real lady — you might say a great lady. The likes of a stock detective never would have seen her before.'

Well, that was putting Pat Reagan in his place. Mrs. Albert, great lady or not, had herself a champion in the Box-A foreman.

The little tiff — real or imagined, I couldn't tell which — ended. Vic Schuyler grinned and everything was fine again. 'How about another little drink?' he said, nodding at the cup.

I declined and he went back in the kitchen for a refill. I decided it was time to start our conversation out in a new direction.

'You don't happen to know a pair of gun sharks that might hire out to do a job of killing, do you?' I said.

'Not more than forty or fifty,' he

called. 'The ranchers have been healing theirselves up with jaspers like that since rustlin' trouble started. Why?'

'How about one who favors brass knucks?'

'In Texas?'

'In New Orlando.'

He came back in the room.

'So that's how you got that face. I've kind of wondered.' He sat down, shaking his head. 'I know most of the leather slappers in these parts. I don't know anybody that favors knucks.'

I mentioned their names, but that didn't help either.

'It happened on Main Street. Maybe they didn't want to disturb the Sheriff by shooting me.'

The foreman shrugged. 'Might be.'

'I figured they knew I was an Association man and somebody doesn't like Association men.'

Shrug.

'How did they know, though? That's what gets me.'

'I knew' he said.

'You were just guessing. Killing a man on a guess is laying it on pretty heavy, even in New Orlando.'

The foreman's eyes were puzzled. 'You sure they were out to kill you?'

'As sure as I'll ever be of anything. They would have done it too, if a stable-man hadn't stepped in with a scatter gun and scared them off.'

'What did they look like?'

I tried to describe them, but it wasn't any good. Vic Schuyler kept shaking his head in that puzzled way. 'They could be any of twenty or thirty men I know, or a thousand men I don't know. They probably came up from the border, though. I've seen knucks downthere.'

'Well, that's something. I'd kind of like to meet up with those gents again.'

The foreman sat there mauling an idea around in his mind. Finally he drained his cup and got up. 'Knucks!' he said. 'By God, let me know when the trouble starts. I'm pretty good at that kind of thing.'

3

About six o'clock the next morning Vic Schuyler ate his breakfast and rode off to look for strays. I broke out my war bag, found my razor with the nick in it, and began tearing the beard off my face. It was time I stopped looking like a stock detective and made myself presentable.

By eight o'clock the mercury was already beginning to nudge 90. By noon you could bake potatoes in the air space between the top of your skull and the crown of your Stetson. I hated to face that sun but I felt like I ought to be doing something to earn my keep.

What I did was get Dusty saddled and take a ride up to the Box-A's north range, looking for clues. Or a piece of shade. What I found was nothing. Then we headed east for a while, and there I found something, George Albert's blonde-haired daughter, Jane, and Kyle Northern.

There was a pool of water and some cool-looking cottonwoods. Down at one end of the pool some cows were stamping around in the water to get it good and muddy before they took a drink. Northern and the girl were up at the other end.

It looked like they were having a picnic. There was a white cloth spread out with chuck all over it. Back behind them there was a stripped-down surrey and a fine light team of bays hitched to some brush. It looked like a fine party, but I hadn't been invited. I was about to turn around and see what else I could find when Northern stood up and called for me to come over.

'This is something of a coincidence,' Northern said. 'We were just talking about you.'

'I don't suppose anything complimentary was said, was there?'

Northern laughed a nice, easy laugh that matched his eyes. 'As a matter of fact we hadn't got around to that. Jane was just telling me that you were a stock detective.'

It took a minute for it to hit me, but when it did hit me I was mad. And there was nothing I could do about it. I looked at Jane Albert, and she smiled sweetly and said, 'I do hope I haven't done anything wrong, Mr. Reagan. It wasn't meant to be a secret, was it?'

'Well,' I said, 'it doesn't make much difference now, does it?' I would like to have climbed down and batted her right between those pretty blue eyes. But instead, I smiled, and she smiled, and Kyle Northern smiled. I said, 'Would you mind telling me how many people know I'm a stock detective?'

'Oh,' she said, 'no one but Kyle and myself. And Marcia and Father, of course. Oh, yes, the feed man came out from New Orlando this morning . . . I'm afraid I may have said something about it to him.' Her eyes widened. 'Do you think he'll tell anybody?'

'Nobody but his customers, probably,' I said. 'But don't worry about it. What fun is there in having a secret if you keep it a secret? By the way, how did you find out?'

'Why, Marcia told me.'

'I don't suppose it would do any good to ask how Marcia found out.'

'I'm sure I don't know. Do you want me to ask her?'

'Never mind,' I said. 'The next time I'll just wear a badge and save confusion all around.'

Northern was paying close attention, trying to figure out if I was mad or not. 'Is it going to make things more difficult for you, Reagan?' he said. 'This business of people knowing who you are?'

'It would have come out sooner or later, anyway.' I began to get over my mad spell. 'Maybe it will even work out better this way. At least everybody will be getting an honest shake.'

Jane Albert, not to be kept out of things for long, said, 'Won't you join us, Mr. Reagan?'

I was tired gabbling, and besides I was hungry. So I surprised them both by saying, 'All right, if you're sure it's not going to put you out any.'

Kyle Northern wasn't crazy about the

idea, but he took it like a man. I unbitted Dusty and let him graze. I ate most of the chicken, and all the bread, and a good part of the potato salad. Kyle Northern smiled through it all.

'I didn't expect to find a place like this,' I said, nodding at the water hole. 'What is it, an underground spring?'

'That's right,' Northern said. 'It's the beginning of Hound Dog Creek. The stream bends in a horseshoe west of my place and plays out near the badlands.'

'Does it go through Phillips' ranch?'

'Why, yes, it does. Why do you ask?'

'I'm just trying to get the lay of the land. The creek goes through the three big ranches near New Orlando. Do outsiders ever try to move in on your water rights?'

'They used to, but that was a long time ago, when I was just a boy. The three big outfits in New Orlando now are too tough for them to go up against.'

'But not too tough for the rustlers?'

'It would seem that way.'

'George Albert thinks one of the

51

ranchers — maybe several of them — are in the thing. Maybe they meant to take over all the land along Hound Dog Creek. They couldn't do it by range wars, so they've decided to steal you blind. Have you got any ideas about that?'

Kyle Northern was getting interested. He was even forgetting to make calf eyes at Jane Albert. 'That's my idea to start with,' he said. 'I think it's clear enough that a rancher is backing the rustlers. How else would they know where to strike all the time?'

'I've heard about Kurt Basser. Does he fit into the picture?'

'He would if he could. But he's too small.'

'Cut out the small ranchers,' I said, 'and what have you got? You, and Albert, and Ran Phillips.'

He didn't say anything. He just sat there looking at me, and maybe a full minute went by before the thing fell on me. It was pretty big to handle at first. By just sitting there and saying nothing, Kyle Northern was implying that one of the Big Three was trying to run the other two out of New Orlando.

It took Jane Albert a little longer to get it. But after a while she did. 'Why, Kyle, what a thing to say! You don't really think Ran would stoop to stealing cows, do you? Of course, I know he needs money, but — well, I just don't think a Phillips would do a thing like that.'

But she had put the words in Northern's mouth, if not the thought. She looked at me.

'Of course,' she said, 'you know what the Phillipses are.'

'I'm not sure,' I said. 'What do you say they are?'

'Well' — and she was half smiling, keeping one of those blue eyes cocked on Northern — 'well, Ran's father, of course, was one of the Richmond Phillipses. A very old Virginia family. It has been a family of planters and gentlemen for generations. Now, really, Mr. Reagan, do you think the son of a fine old family would stoop to stealing cows?'

'Fine old things have a way of falling,' I

said. 'But I didn't suggest that Ran Phillips was behind the rustling. You did.'

She frowned, but she wasn't angry. 'Why, Mr. Reagan, I did no such thing!'

I tore up my original estimate of Jane Albert and began to draw up a new one. She was really quite a girl, aside from her looks. It was pretty clear that she liked Northern, but it was also clear that she liked to bait him with that 'fine old Virginia family' of Ran Phillips — and Northern jumped at it.

I don't know what makes some women like that. They nag their husbands to death and then grieve themselves into an early grave when they're gone. Whatever it was, Jane Albert was doing a pretty good job on Kyle Northern. She would never let him forget that he was nothing but a common brush popper, no matter how hard he worked and how many cows he owned. You can't buy family line.

Northern still hadn't said anything, but he looked as if some of that fried chicken was going bad in his stomach. I could feel a storm coming up, and I didn't think I wanted to be around when it hit.

'Well, I'd better mosey along,' I said. 'Everybody's going to expect me to look like a stock detective from here on out.'

Jane Albert smiled. If I had looked close enough maybe I could have read something into it. Maybe even an invitation. 'I do hope I haven't made things inconvenient for you, Mr. Reagan.'

'I get paid to take care of inconveniences,' I said. Northern said the usual things while I got saddled up, but his mind wasn't on it. There was a grim set to his jaw and I got the idea that he was still thinking of that 'fine old Virginia family.' He should have known better than to let things like that get under his skin, but I felt sorry for him just the same.

'By the way,' I said, when I was in the saddle, 'when was the last raid the rustlers made?'

'Almost two weeks ago. They got away with twenty head of my beef steers, just a beginning of a herd I was gathering for the trail.'

'Any way of guessing when they'll hit again?' He shrugged.

'Well, I'll be seeing you, Northern. Good-bye, Miss Albert.'

She and Northern watched me ride down to the far end of the pool. I wasn't even out of hearing distance when the argument started.

★ ★ ★

Well, now that everybody had me spotted as a detective, I felt like I ought to start acting like one. Let's see, what did I have to work with? First, there was a man named Basser somewhere in the picture. He had been responsible for lynching a pair of night riders, and as a consequence nothing much had been learned about their employer. That was enough to put Basser in a bad light. But everybody seemed to agree that his caliber was too small for him to be the boss of anything.

Well, there was Phillips. Northern and Jane Albert had practically accused him

56

of ramrodding the thing, but that wasn't much to go on. Maybe I ought to talk to Phillips, though. . . . Who else was there? Oh, yes, there was Northern himself, an ambitious man if I ever saw one. Worked himself from brush popper to a big ranch owner in the span of a few years. Maybe he wasn't through yet. Maybe he was putting his chips on all or nothing.

Maybe.

How about my pals, Huck and Kramer? I had an idea they could tell me a lot of interesting things if I ever got the chance to put the question to them. But maybe that wasn't going to be in the cards. Who else? There was George Albert, but I couldn't very well go around accusing my boss of rustling. Anyway, he was the one who had written for help.

I added all that up and it didn't come to anything to speak of. All I knew for sure was that somebody was stealing an Association member's cattle.

I tried to think of something else. Well, there was Jane Albert. She didn't have anything to do with the rustling, of course, but she was kind of interesting to think about. With those innocent blue eyes, and that gentle smile, and that small, almost timid voice. A bitch-wolf, if I ever saw one, but her disguise was near perfect. Poor Kyle Northern.

That about took in everybody I had met since coming to New Orlando, except the stableman, Vic Schuyler, and Marcia Albert.

Marcia Albert!

It came right out of nowhere, the way forgotten things do sometime. I jerked up in the saddle as if the wind had been knocked out of me. Finally I remembered.

It had taken some time, but I finally had her pegged now. *Marcia Albert.* Except, of course, her name hadn't been Albert when I knew her. It hadn't been Marcia, either, for that matter. What had it been?

Abigail? No, that was another one. Beatrice? Della? Harriet? That was it — Harriet. Harriet Somebody . . . Maybe she hadn't even had a last name in those days!

I sat back in the saddle and laughter rolled into the big, hot afternoon. Well, I'll be damned!

I must have looked like an idiot, riding around in circles and braying like a lovesick jackass. But I had to let off steam some way. The last time I saw Marcia Albert she had been the belle of the Bull's Head Saloon in Abilene. Poor old Vic Schuyler! *She's a real lady — you might say a great lady! Came from back East somewhere!*

That started me laughing all over again.

The Kansas railheads were as far east as Marcia Albert had ever been. If you bought wine at four dollars a throw, she would sit on your lap and chuck you under the chin with one hand while she lifted your trail pay with the other. That was Harriet of the Bull's Head, all right. Or Marcia, rather. And a nicer lapful a trail-dirty drover never held. She had had looks in those days too, although her face had been smeared with paint like any other trail-town fancy girl.

Then I stopped laughing. Suddenly it was no longer funny. It was a little sad. I didn't know how she had managed to land a man like George Albert — but land him she had. Maybe she even loved him. Anyway, it wasn't any of my business.

I remembered the whiteness of her face when I had brushed her off for a common saloon girl the day before. I thought it had been rage and indignation at the time, but now I knew it was fear. I knew a saloon girl instinctively. I could tell one with my eyes closed. That was the thing that got her.

Only George Albert had taken it as a perfectly legitimate mistake, so that meant that he didn't know about her past.

Well, he wasn't going to find out from me. I had enough to worry about without getting mixed up in somebody's family affairs. And Vic Schuyler could go on thinking that he was working for a great lady if he wanted to. The hell with all of them. I was beginning to wish for a way to ease out of New Orlando and forget the whole thing.

Then I thought of something else.

Jane Albert said Marcia had told her I was a stock detective. Had Marcia recognized me the same as I had recognized her, or had George Albert told her about me? I couldn't even make a guess about that one.

There's no telling how long I would have kept going in circles if I hadn't spotted the dust cloud rising up in the east. I rode over to a knoll and saw that it was Vic Schuyler and some of his riders moving a herd up from the south. The foreman waved to me and yelled something that I couldn't catch, so I thought I might as well ride down and see what was going on.

I watched the cattle mill around as the sweating, cursing riders tried to move them over to the west. Around five hundred head, good beef steers around three or four years old. The foreman nudged his horse away from the herd and came over.

'Hot as hell,' he shouted. 'You didn't

bring my jug along, did you?'

'I didn't think of it. Somebody snake-bit?'

'A man gets thirsty,' he said. 'Catch any rustlers yet?'

'Not yet. I've been up at the spring eating fried chicken with Jane Albert and her man.'

'Which one?'

'Which man? Has she got more than one?'

'Every pup in New Orlando sniffing around, I guess. Mostly just two, though. Phillips and Northern.'

'It was Northern this time.'

'If you stay around long enough,' Schuyler said, 'you'll probably see one of them buried. Phillips or Northern, that is.'

'I got to watch her technique for a while,' I said. 'It was pretty good. Northern and Phillips seemed friendly enough, though, when I met them yesterday.'

The foreman snorted. 'The boss — old man Albert, that is — tries to keep the big ranchers pulled together. They don't blaze up much when he's around.' He wiped his face on the sleeve of his red underwear. 'Days like this, damn if I don't wish I was back in Dakota. If you're not doin' anything, why don't you wait till we get this bunch of beef bedded down and I'll ride back to the ranch house with you.'

'All right,' I said. 'Where are you taking them?'

'Up by the creek. Our south range is all grazed out, so we had to move them.'

'Is this all of the Box-A herd?'

'Hell, no. Two more herds about the same size, one east and one south. We have to keep movin' them around.'

The foreman went back to the herd, then I joined in and we all yelled and shouted and cursed until we finally got the cattle where we wanted them. Schuyler stationed a night watch of five men and the rest of us headed back for the home range.

Vic Schuyler was one of those big riders that you hear about but almost never see. In spite of his weight he could sit a saddle as light as anybody I ever saw. We talked about different things as we plodded back to the ranch house — mostly about the fine art of making good rye whiskey. We didn't mention the Alberts. I sure didn't mention the fact that I had finally pegged Mrs. Albert in my memory.

As we raised the ranch buildings we could see Northern pulling away in that stripped-down surrey of his. As we pulled up at the home corral and turned our horses over to the wrangler, Jane Albert came out on the front porch and waved at us. I hadn't got to be completely antisocial yet, so I waved back.

'You pretty good with a gun?' Vic Schuyler asked.

'I manage to stay alive, that's about all. Why?'

'Northern and Phillips both have reputations as gun throwers. I just wondered.'

'What brought this on?' I asked. 'Just because I waved at their girl?'

But I guess the foreman figured he had said enough. He pulled out a yard of red bandana and mopped his face. 'By God, this sun gives a man a thirst. You ready?'

I was ready, but about that time Jane Albert called something, so we stopped and she came across the ranch yard toward us.

'Oh, Mr. Reagan, I just want to tell you that Kyle and I enjoyed having you with us this afternoon.'

'Well, that's fine,' I said. 'The next time you've got some chuck you want to get rid of, just give me a call.'

'That's just what I'm doing,' she smiled. 'Father wants you to have supper with us tonight at the ranch house. . . . And Mr. Schuyler, too. If he doesn't have something else to do, that is.'

I couldn't tell what the foreman thought of it. Personally, I wasn't crazy about the idea of facing Marcia, now that I knew who she was. But at the moment I couldn't think of any graceful way of bowing out.

I said, 'Well, there's nothing like getting fattened up for the kill, I guess.'

She grinned as if she knew what I was

talking about, which was more than I knew. 'Six o'clock,' she said. 'It's nothing special, so don't go to any trouble.' She turned and ran like a scared antelope back to the front porch.

I looked at the foreman. 'What do you think?'

'I think, by God, we ought to do something about that drink.'

So that was what we did. We got the vinegar jug out and filled up the tin cups. After the third time around, the world began to look like a fit place to live in.

'What happens when you get invited to supper at the ranch house?' I asked. 'Maybe we ought to change our socks or something.'

'You couldn't prove it by me,' the foreman said. 'I never was invited before. Not to take any meals.' He waved the jug. 'Here, let me fill her up.'

'Let me catch my breath for a minute. What do you think Albert wants to see us about?'

Schuyler snorted. 'He probably don't know we're coming yet. It's that girl.' He looked at me over his cup. 'This ain't nothin' personal, of course, but I think she's about to put her brand on you.'

'What's the matter, can't two men keep her busy?'

Snort again.

'Maybe we shouldn't go.'

The foreman wiped his mouth thoughtfully. 'Well . . . I wouldn't say that.'

4

It was six o'clock by Vic Schuyler's turnip when we tramped up to the front porch, hair combed, boots wiped, a change of outer clothes, more or less clean, shaved, rubbed down with a bucket of cold well water. It seemed a shame to waste all that grooming on just a supper. We were good for a funeral, at least.

George Albert seemed slightly puzzled by it all, but naturally good manners kept him from throwing us out after we explained that it was his daughter's idea. Then Jane Albert came in looking like the picture on the cover of Codey's Lady's Book. Something in black, as I remember, dragging the Boor and fitting like the skin on a peach. No hoop skirts for Jane Albert. Through a whiskey haze I could see white shoulders — a lot of white shoulders.

I don't know where she got the dress, but probably it was a hangover from that

Mississippi trip of hers. Nobody in Texas would make a dress like that. It reminded me of those portraits you see of the great Civil War ladies of the Old South, when décolleté was the latest thing in women's fashions.

George Albert looked a little shocked, but I guess he had learned to keep his mouth shut. It was quite an effort, though. He looked as if he would like to turn his daughter over a sawhorse and tan her backside with a stick of stove wood. He looked as if he might do it too, someday.

I don't remember what we talked about. About the rustling, I suppose. Jane Albert didn't say much of anything. She just sat and smiled, like a statue on exhibition.

Vic Schuyler sat uncomfortably on the edge of a chair, frowning at the mounted buffalo head over the fireplace. He was waiting for something. I didn't know what it was until she came in, and then I knew it was Marcia Albert.

'How do you do, Mr. Reagan? Mr. Schuyler?'

Very nice and polite. The words were edged with a little frost, but nobody noticed it except me. She had learned a lot of things since her days at the Bull's Head Saloon.

Vic Schuyler lunged to his feet. His face was as red as a Missouri barn.

That, I guess, was when it hit me that the big foreman was in love with Marcia Albert. At first I thought I must be mistaken. But it was no mistake. It was in his eyes, in everything he did. Not a lustful love, or a covetous love, just a nice quiet kind of insanity.

I don't think Marcia Albert even noticed. She looked right past the foreman, at me.

'How do you do, Mrs. Albert?' I said. She seemed to expect something else, so I added, 'It's nice of you to ask us to supper.'

'Jane did the planning,' she said, half-smiling all around. 'However, I'm sure that Mr. Albert and myself are quite as pleased as Jane that you could come.'

This was something! No bawdy-house

manners at the Box-A.

'I think it's silly,' Jane Albert said, 'that Mr. Reagan shouldn't stay here in the ranch house, now that we know he's a range detective.'

'Range detectives are not always the nicest people,' I said, grinning.

Marcia looked at me. I couldn't tell what she was thinking. 'It must be exciting being a range detective,' she said. 'You must get to a lot of places.'

'Yes,' I said, 'we do that, all right.' 'Have you ever been to Abilene?'

The atmosphere seemed to frost over just a little as she looked at me, and I knew then that she had recognized me. If I had been smart I would have said, 'No, ma'am, I never saw Abilene in my life,' and we'd have smiled and that would have been the end of it. But that wasn't my moment to be smart. I said, 'Yes, ma'am, I know Abilene pretty well.'

A pair of little shutters closed behind those dark eyes of hers. She didn't even lose her smile. 'Jane, darling,' she said, 'will you see if supper's ready yet?'

* * *

It must have been a good supper, but I didn't notice. I sat there stuffing food in my mouth and wishing I could think of a way to get out of there. I was vaguely aware of Vic Schuyler being miserably uncomfortable and dropping food in his lap out of sheer nervousness. But every once in a while he would sneak a glance at Marcia Albert, and that seemed to make up for everything. After dessert George Albert brought some brandy out and Schuyler tossed it off the same as he downed that rye of his.

I guess that was enough for Albert. He started yawning and saying that he had had a hard day, which maybe he had. Any day would be a hard day with women like that on your hands.

There was the usual talk at the door, with George Albert and Marcia artfully fading out of it and disappearing. Jane Albert came out on the porch with us.

'Well, good night, Miss Albert,' Vic Schuyler said.

'Good night, Vic.'

The foreman waited a minute to see if I was going to play it smart and come with him. It wasn't my day to be smart. He grunted and marched off into the darkness.

There was a sweet, heavy scent of honeysuckle in the night air. I said, 'Do you feel like talking for a while?'

'I love to talk, Mr. Reagan.' She leaned against me and there was a smell of rose water in her hair. 'What do you want to talk about?'

'Maybe this isn't very appropriate, but I'd like to hear some more about Ran Phillips. You practically indicted him on a rustling charge this afternoon, you know.'

She smiled. 'There's a swing at the end of the porch. Would you like to sit down?'

It was one of those two-passenger swings that hang by chains from the porch rafters and usually squeal like a pig under a fence when you sit in them. This one didn't squeal. She moved over close.

'Now what was it you wanted to talk about?'

'Phillips, remember?'

'Oh, Ran never did anything. I told you that. I just talk about Ran because Kyle gets so mad. He's sweet when he's mad.'

'He's going to get one of those sweet-moods some day and cut somebody's heart out. Maybe yours.'

She laughed and snuggled closer. 'Let's don't talk about them. Let's talk about you. Have you known many women?'

'Yes. Now, let's hear about Phillips.'

She sat up, pouting. 'Well,' she said coldly, 'you leave Ran alone. Why, he's from a fine old Virginia family and he wouldn't ever do anything that wasn't right.'

'Are you in love with him?' I asked.

'That's none of your business.'

'How about Kyle Northern?'

'That's none of your business, either. If you're just going to sit here and ask questions, I think I'll go back in the house.'

But she didn't move. I pulled her over, tilted her head back and kissed her. She was a little cool at first. But not for long.

'Well,' I said. That seemed to be all I could think of.

'Your face is almost well,' she said. 'I think I'm going to like you.'

'I don't think I want to be around when you really make up your mind. What are your boyfriends going to think about this, anyway?'

'Do they have to know?'

'You'll probably tell them, just to watch the pretty blue flame when they burn,' I said.

She laughed. 'You don't like me very much, do you?'

'Not very.'

'Kiss me, Pat. Your name is Pat, isn't it?'

'That's right,' I said.'

A girl really ought to know a man's first name, I guess.'

A good deal of time must have gone by. Time has a way of getting away from you at times like that. I broke it up and said, 'What about Northern? He's not so filthy with money that he couldn't dirty himself a little more, is he?'

She pushed me away. 'You make me mad!'

She sulked awhile, but she didn't go away. How did George Albert ever come by a daughter like that, anyway?

'Well, what about your stepmother?' I said.

'What about her?' she pouted.

'Anything at all. How do you like her? Where did your father meet her? Anything you want to tell me.'

'Marcia's all right,' she said finally. She doesn't try to boss me around — I was afraid she would when I came home from Mississippi, but she didn't. Father met her in St. Louis, I think. She was a friend of some cattle buyers that he knew. They got married kind of sudden and came back to Texas without a honeymoon or anything. That's the way Marcia wanted it.'

She paused for a moment, the tip of her tongue tracing the edge of her red mouth. 'I'm glad they got married,' she said abruptly. 'Father was lonely here on the ranch by himself, and I never was much help. I've caused him quite a bit of worry, I guess.'

I listened to horses stamping nervously in the darkness. Away in the distance a coyote barked. A thin slice of a moon hung low over the prairie, looking pale and lonesome.

After a while I realized that Jane Albert was through talking. She sat there for a few minutes, that pink tongue licking between her parted lips. She seemed to have forgotten that I was sitting there. Then, without saying a word, she got up and went into the house.

I sat there for some time, thinking that she had just gone after a handkerchief or something and in a minute she would be back. She didn't come back. I rolled two cigarettes and burned them up. Nothing happened.

I got up, walked over to the front steps and rolled another cigarette. It seemed that I could smell roses, but it was Jane

Albert still running around in my memory.

I decided to wait a few more minutes, just in case. The house was dark. No sound came from it, but I could imagine that I heard the measured breathing of sleeping people. George Albert dreaming about his stolen cattle, probably. Or maybe he was lying awake, thinking how lucky he was to have a beautiful young wife like Marcia. Jane Albert — God alone could guess what she was doing or thinking.

Well, I thought, it's time to go home.

Then I wheeled as if somebody had stabbed me with an icicle, and there she was, standing in the screened doorway. Not Jane Albert. Marcia.

She wasn't doing anything that I could see. Just standing there like a pale ghost, watching me with those dark eyes. After a while my heart started beating again. There was no expression at all on that pale face as she opened the screen and floated onto the porch.

'What do you want?' she said.

'Am I supposed to want something,

Harriet?'

'My name is Mrs. George Albert,' she said coldly. 'If it's money you want, I can get some for you. Not much, but some.'

'I don't want any money,' I said. 'I don't want anything. Let's just forget the past, Mrs. Albert. Do you want to? We'll just pretend I met you yesterday, and let it go at that.' I started backing off.

'Wait a minute,' she said.

She came forward, stopping not more than two or three inches from me. She tilted her chin back, breathing lightly through her mouth. 'You know me,' she said tightly. 'You know about Abilene, and the Bull's Head, and all the rest of it.'

I didn't say anything.

'I'm glad you came,' she said, her voice suddenly soft. 'Don't you think I'm glad? Don't you think I almost go crazy here, with nothing to do but listen to this eternal prairie wind, feeling myself bake out and grow old in this everlasting sun?'

I couldn't make a sound.

'I remember you, too,' she said. 'You

used to come to the Bull's Head. Remember the good times we had there? I want to feel young again, the way I felt then.'

Her hands touched the front of my shirt. They went around my neck, and my mouth got dry and I began to have trouble swallowing.

'For God's sake,' I said, 'what about your husband?'

She made a little sound — a laugh, I guess it was supposed to be. 'He's twice as old as I am. What kind of husband do you think that is? Anyway, he's asleep. Sound a sleep . . .

That was when I felt it.

It wasn't much at first. Just a little sting, like a bee sitting down between my shoulder blades. It wasn't much, but it was enough. It brought me out of my trance. I wasn't very gentle about it.

I jerked a knee up and slammed it in her stomach. I grabbed her hair and jerked her head back. Then I hacked down on her arm and the knife went clattering to the porch.

I was wound up, I guess. I couldn't

stop. I don't like for women to stick knives in my back while they make love to me.

Marcia Albert was about to go to her knees when I caught her. I dragged her over to the swing and stretched her out. Her mouth was working, trying to get some air into her lungs, and she was as sick as she would ever be and keep living. In the day-light her face would have been green.

I went over and picked up the knife. It was an ordinary kitchen knife, but plenty long enough and sharp enough to puncture a man's gizzard. I didn't know how she hid it — probably in the sleeve of that wrap-around she wore. Not that it made any difference now.

'All right,' I said. 'Now what was the idea of pulling a trick like that?'

Then she began to cry. It sounded like crying, but there were no tears that I could see. Pretty soon it was over.

'I'll kill you,' she said hoarsely. 'I'll kill you yet. You'll never tell him.'

'Tell your husband about your Kansas days? Didn't I say once that all that was in the past?'

'You didn't mean it. You'll tell him. You will, when you get all the money out of me that I can give you. I knew it when I first saw you.'

She was getting hysterical. Her voice was getting higher and higher and pretty soon she was going to start screaming and then there was going to be hell to pay.

I grabbed her shoulders and shook her. I said, 'Listen to me. Do you want to wake your husband?'

That did it. She was suddenly calm.

'Now get these damn fool ideas out of your head,' I said. 'I don't want your money or anything else. I especially don't want any more knives in my back. If morals was my business I'd be a preacher, not a stock detective. It doesn't make a damn to me what you were before you married George Albert. Now see if you can get that through your head.'

She looked at me hard, blinking her eyes. Then she began to cry again. Really cry this time.

This was sure one hell of a family that George Albert had gathered around him. One thing could be said for him, though. He had a wife that loved him so much that she would kill to keep him. If that was any consolation.

'I'm just tired,' Marcia Albert said between sobs. 'Tired to death.'

At first I thought she was talking about our scuffle, but then I understood that it was something else.

'It's not very easy, is it?' I said. 'Changing over from one kind of life to another?'

I didn't expect an answer and I didn't get one.

'Well, I'm here to worry about stolen cattle and nothing else,' I went on. 'Keep that in mind the next time you get your hands on a knife. How do you feel?'

'All right.'

'You're going to be a little stove up in the morning. What are you going to tell your husband?'

'I'll explain it somehow.'

'I'll bet. You could have explained the body on your front porch too, couldn't you, if I hadn't taken that knife away from you?'

No answer to that one.

I was suddenly tired. It was quite a night, but I'd seen enough. I walked away and left Marcia Albert there on the porch swing and headed across the ranch yard toward the foreman's house. I wondered what she was going to tell her husband if he woke up and found her missing.

She'd think of something. I discovered that I still had the knife in my hand. I threw it as hard as I could into the darkness.

Vic Schuyler was in bed when I came in, but he hadn't gone to sleep. I fumbled around until I got a lamp lit, and there he was resting on his elbow, frowning at me. 'By God,' he said, 'what happened to you, anyway?'

'Nothing that ten or twenty years of clean living won't smooth over. Have you got any more of that snake poison?'

'Sure. In the kitchen.'

There was a jug half-full in the kitchen

safe, along with five full ones. Vic was looking forward to a hard winter, I guess. I filled a tin cup and gulped it down. Sparks flew when it hit my stomach, but after a while it took hold and my nerves stopped playing tug-of-war and I began to relax.

All I wanted was to go to bed. Tomorrow I'd get up early and pamper my nerves by breaking wild horses, or picking a gun fight with somebody. Anything, just so it didn't include women.

It must have been around midnight when I finally got peeled down and went to sleep. But that wasn't my night. About an hour later the shooting started and woke me up again.

5

It was a long way off and not loud at all. If it had been any other kind of noise I would have slept right on through it. But gunfire and sleep, like oil and water, just won't mix.

I snapped up in bed and heard Vic Schuyler cursing and fumbling around in the darkness for his clothes. I found my shirt, got a match out of the pocket and lit the lamp. I began to pull my pants on and called, 'Sounds like we've got company.'

The foreman cursed some more. He flung the door open and bellowed into the darkness. After a minute some-body — the cook, I guess — began pounding on the dinner gong. I jerked my boots on and went into the front room buckling my gun belt.

'Rustlers?' I said.

'The sons-of-bitches always have to come at night!' He grunted angrily.

86

'They sound a long way off.'

'Down on the south range,' he said. 'They're either in our herds or Northern's. Both outfits have got cows down there.'

We went out of the house at a run and headed across the ranch yard toward the barns. The bunkhouse was ablaze with lamplight, and figures were scurrying around in the darkness yelling where the hell was the wrangler. Then the barn lit up, and the saddle shed, and then there was lamplight in the ranch house. Everybody grabbed a saddle — anybody's saddle — and started cutting the best horses out of the holding corral. I found Dusty and started buckling leather on him.

Vic Schuyler was already saddled up and was directing things in that bull voice of his. The wrangler was interested only in getting a fast-looking little bay rigged out — the boss's horse, I guessed. Sure enough, here came George Albert running across the ranch yard. 'That's the south range, isn't it, Vic?' he called.

'That's right,' Vic Schuyler said. 'They're either in our beef or Northern's, I guess.'

'Well, by God,' George Albert said, 'we'll get them this time. We can bring our riders and Northern's together. Probably Phillips' as well. They're not going to drive off any cattle with that many men shooting at them.'

He climbed on the little bay and looked around. 'All ready, Vic?'

'All ready.'

'Then let's go!'

We lit out of the ranch yard, about a dozen of us altogether, and headed for the open spaces to the south. We rode for about ten minutes and then pulled up to see if we could still hear the firing. We could.

'Sounds like it's west of Northern's place,' Vic Schuyler said. 'That would put them somewhere between Northern and Phillips.'

'Well, what are we waiting on?'

We lit out again, and this time we didn't stop until we saw the flashes of their guns. We were on a small knoll and the shooting was going on down by the bend in the creek. It looked like a regular battle, with all the uproar and the dozens of muzzle flashes stabbing at the night.

'It sure as hell looks like they brought an army with them this time,' the foreman said. 'That must be the night guard down on the creek.'

So we headed for the creek. A lanky, powder-smelling cowhand came stumbling up the draw to meet us. 'It sure looks like hell's broke loose this time,' he said. 'What outfit you people from?'

'The Box-A,' George Albert said. 'Who are you?'

'We was Kyle Northern's night guard until we got hell shot out of us. They jumped us a while back on the other side of the creek. They hit us from ambush. I know it sounds crazy, but that's what they did. I don't know what they're up to, unless they meant to kill the night guard and then ride off with the beef.'

The shooting had quieted down for

a minute. The men were picketing their horses in the draw and taking up positions along the bank.

I said, 'Did you lose any men?'

'I don't think so,' Northern's rider said. 'I don't know how they missed us, though. There must be at least twenty of them, from the way they were shooting. Herd's scattered to hell and gone.'

One of the rustlers got impatient. A rifle cracked and a bullet ripped through the brush and whopped into the mud on the opposite bank of the creek. Then the night exploded. It sounded like a battalion had opened up on us. We all ducked, and some of the men took pot shots at the flashes.

Then we heard horses. They entered the draw to the west of us and came down to where we were. It was Northern and his riders.

'Hello, Reagan,' Northern said. 'What's going on here?'

'The third battle of Bull Run, from the looks of things,' I said. I pointed down the creek to where the stream twisted.

'That's where they are, I think. About twenty of them, your men say. When they start shooting it looks like twice that many.'

Northern called his men together and got them lined up on the bank. 'Well, they'll catch hell pretty soon,' he said. 'Phillips and his riders ought to be here any minute.'

The rustlers let us have another volley, and that quieted things down for a while. Then we heard more horses in the draw. This time it was Ran Phillips.

I lay on the bank and watched the fireworks while Albert and Phillips and Northern held a powwow down the draw. There was no sense in wasting six-gun cartridges at that distance. For that matter, there wasn't much sense in rifles either, because you couldn't see anything to shoot at but Hashes. Vic Schuyler crawled up beside me with a saddle gun.

'This is the damnedest thing I ever saw,' I said.

'What do you mean?'

'Well, the rustlers sure aren't going to

get any cattle stolen by laying behind a creek bank and taking pot shots at us. Still, it can't very well be a decoy. Not with that many men.'

'You figure it out,' Vic Schuyler said. 'I'm goin' to do a little shootin'.'

He emptied his magazine at the flashes. We couldn't see whether he had hit anything or not. There was loud talk down the draw where the Big Three confab was taking place, but I couldn't catch much of it because of all the shooting.

Then Kyle Northern called out, 'Reagan, come here a minute, will you?'

I climbed down the bank and Albert said, 'What do you think about it, Reagan?'

'Well, with a few more men I'd say you had a pretty good chance to get yourself some rustlers.'

'I guess that settles it,' Albert said. 'We'll call in our night guard, and as soon as we've got the man- power we'll trap them in the creek.'

'Isn't that going to leave your herds pretty naked?' I asked.

'Look at that shooting,' Ran Phillips said. 'We've got the whole band down there. I say, do a good job while we're at it and clean them out.'

They all nodded, as if they were glad to be able to agree on something. 'Keep up the shooting, boys,' George Albert called. 'We don't want to give them a chance of getting away.' And about that time the rustlers let go another barrage. They didn't seem to be in any hurry.

I went back to my own personal fortress beside Vic Schuyler.

'What did they decide?' Vic asked.

'They're going to call in the night guard and capture themselves some rustlers. So they say.'

He thought about it for a minute. 'You don't think so?'

'It'll be leaving a lot of cattle to take care of themselves.'

The foreman shrugged. 'What the hell? As long as we've got the rustlers pinned down here.'

It seemed that I was outvoted. Maybe I was getting too careful in my old age, but I had learned that two and two didn't always make four — not when a cow thief was at the blackboard. Just on a hunch, though, I couldn't very well set out to talk three big ranchers out of a scheme that might end all their worries.

Time went by. We kept popping back and forth at each other and not getting anywhere. But that was about all we could do until the reinforcements came up.

I don't know just when it was that I began to get the feeling that something was wrong. Something was missing. I thought about it for a long while before anything happened. It was an uncomfortable feeling, like finding yourself way out on ice and seeing it break off all around you. We kept popping back and forth, and once in a while the rustlers would let go with a volley that rocked the landscape.

Finally it hit me. 'Well, by God!' Vic Schuyler looked at me.

'There's something wrong here,' I said. 'Wrong as hell. Haven't you noticed it?'

'I noticed we're getting shot at. That's wrong enough for me.'

'The shooting,' I said. 'That's the funny thing about it. Wait a minute.' I stood up and shouted, 'Give them another round, boys. Let them know we're still here.'

The cowhands all burned a cartridge or two. Then, sure enough, the rustlers all turned loose with a volley of their own.

Vic Schuyler ducked his head. 'I've lost my sense of humor maybe,' he grunted, 'but right now nothin' strikes me very funny.'

'It's the bullets,' I said. 'There aren't any. Damn few, anyway.'

His head snapped around. 'Maybe you ought to get some rest.'

'It's a fact. Look, we'll do it all over again. You listen and see if you hear any bullets.' I raised up and yelled, 'Do it again, boys!'

We did. There was a big explosion when the rustlers turned loose, but the zip of bullets wasn't there.

The foreman's eyes bugged. 'Well, I'll

be damned!'

'What do you think?' I said.

'The same thing you're thinking, probably,' he said hoarsely. He suddenly turned loose and rolled down the bank, yelling for George Albert.

The Box-A boss appeared around a bend in the creek, cradling a carbine in the crook of his arm.

'What's wrong here?'

Vic Schuyler looked as if he was going to be sick. 'Boss,' he said, 'we've got to get out of here. We've got to get back to those herds before it's too late. If it's not too late already.'

George Albert frowned. 'Reagan, can you tell me what my foreman's gibbering about?'

'I think so,' I said. 'It looks like the rustlers laid out the bait and we've jumped at it like a bunch of pilgrims. I don't think there are more than two or three rustlers up there.' I listened. 'Maybe *they're* not there now. I think you'd better take your foreman's advice and look after your herds, if it's not too late.'

I thought I could see Albert's face pale. Then the sound of boots in the draw, and Northern appeared.

'We're ready now,' he said. 'The night guard just came in.'

'You better turn them around!' Vic Schuyler exploded. 'We been gettin' shot at by a bunch of goddam firecrackers. The rustlers've probably got our beef into the badlands by now.'

Phillips rounded the bend in time to get in on the foreman's speech. He stood very still for a minute, looking at Northern. 'Is that right?' he said. 'Did we get suckered down here in the creek?'

'According to Reagan, we did,' Northern said.

'But we've got no time to talk about it now, if we want to save our beef.'

'We've wasted hours,' Phillips said coldly. 'Another minute or two can't hurt us any more. Kyle, wasn't it your idea to draw in the night guard?'

Small fires began to burn behind Northern's eyes. 'Like hell I did!' he said. 'You're the one that was so sure we were going to catch the rustlers here.'

It was time somebody stepped in, but I didn't want the job.

But George Albert could get away with it. He cleared his throat and the two ranchers began to smooth their feathers down. 'Vic,' Albert said, 'you go up the creek and see what you can find.'

The foreman moved away. For a minute or two Northern and Phillips stood there glaring at each other. But you can't draw blood with looks. Phillips hitched his gun belt around to a more handy position and walked away.

'By God, they suckered us, all right!' Vic Schuyler said when he got back from his expedition. He held out a hand and showed a few powder-burned scraps of red paper. 'Firecrackers! Not a soul up there now. They can't be far away, though, if you want to go after them.'

'Never mind that,' George Albert said dully. 'Let's see about the herds.'

We might as well have gone home and got some sleep, because we knew what we were going to find. It was just beginning to be daylight by the time we got back up to George Albert's north range. The herd was so scattered that we couldn't tell how many animals were missing. But some were missing, all right.

'I guess we'd better buy a ticket for the badlands,' I said. 'They can't have too much a start on us. Maybe we can head them off.'

'You don't know the badlands,' George Albert said. 'But I guess you're right. That's the only thing we can do.' He stood up in his stirrups and called to his riders. 'Ike, you and Jordan and Bascome stay here and see if you can get the herd together, what's left of it. When you get a count made, bring it up to the ranch house. Vic, you take the rest and see what you can find. You'd better take Reagan along with you.'

'All right, boss,' Schuyler said. 'Well, let's get started.'

Pretty soon the sun came out as hot as a blacksmith's forge and we began to realize that we hadn't got much sleep the night before. But neither had the rustlers. We kept riding.

Around mid-morning the trail broke up on some hard shale and we wasted an hour cutting for new sign. By that time we were in the badlands — boulders as big as a Kansas City hotel lying out there in the middle of God's nowhere, the harsh red land bursting and cracked, canyons slashing this way and that until you began to think you were in the middle of a Chinese maze. We had to backtrack several times and search around until we found a way to get across those deep gullies. That was where the rustlers had us. They had their trails laid out and knew where they were going, while we had to grope around and fumble like blind souls in Limbo. It was around noon, I guess, when the trail petered out completely.

I couldn't say that I was sorry. I believed what they said about badlands. I'd had enough of it to last a while.

Vic Schuyler just sat on his horse, looking beat and bewildered, when we finally came to the dead end. There was nothing we could do. The cattle were gone, the trail was gone, the men were beginning to doze in their saddles.

'Well,' Vic Schuyler said heavily.

'Maybe we've overlooked something,' I said.

'What?'

'I don't know, but it doesn't stand to reason that a herd of cattle could just disappear.'

'But they did,' the foreman said.

I sighed. 'It looks that way. You want to pick up the trail and start over again?'

'Do you think it would do any good?'

I didn't. We sat there for a while, letting that New Orlando sun dehydrate us; then, without a word, we turned around and headed back for the Box-A

Albert met us as we came in, looking as if he had slept some, but not very much or very well.

'The trail played out,' Schuyler said . . . 'Or maybe we just lost it. Did the others do any good?'

Albert shook his head. 'The others have been back for almost an hour. They didn't see anything. The boys came with the count a little while ago — sixty head missing out of the north herd. Northern says he lost some too, but he doesn't know how many yet. Phillips' herd wasn't bothered.' He smiled weakly. 'Well, I guess we might as well call it a day. Get some rest and we'll thresh it out tomorrow.'

We turned our horses over to the wrangler for feeding and put our saddles in the shed. We were too tired to talk. Vic Schuyler didn't even go to his jug. He dropped on the bunk and began snoring.

That's what I should have done, I guess. I tried, but for some reason sleep wouldn't come. I got up and sampled the foreman's rye whiskey, but not even that helped much. What kind of a thing was this, anyway? I never saw the cow that could walk over ground and not leave a trail of some kind. Even over hard shale. A faint trail maybe — a trail that only very good eyes could see — but God, a trace ought to be there. Wind hadn't blown it away because there hadn't been any wind. What had happened to it?

Where had we missed it?

They were pretty smooth, all right, even for rustlers. Take that firecracker trick. Who would have thought that grown men would be stupid enough to be fooled by a thing like that? The rustlers had. And they had been right. Another thing: how had they known about that herd on the north range? Schuyler had brought it up only that afternoon. Somebody was either a mind reader or he knew exactly how George Albert rotated his herds. Whatever it was, it was smooth. Suckering us down on the creek while they drove off the isolated herd up north.

Back to that firecracker trick, though. I was ashamed of that one. It hurt my professional pride. A man dodging and ducking every time a string of Fourth of July fireworks went off!

By that time I had my clothes on again.

In a few minutes I had a big gelding out and saddled. I headed south.

What I expected to find down there on the creek I don't know. Follow your hunches, though. Hunches were about all I had left. I picketed the gelding and went up the creek to where the fireworks had taken place. Sure enough, the brush was full of exploded pieces of stiff red paper. I gathered up a handful of them, looked at them, smelled them, even stuck out my tongue and tasted one of them. They didn't tell me a thing.

I blundered around a while longer. Boot heels in the soft dirt along the creek bank. They could be anybody's boot heels. A couple of pairs of them, as well as I could make out. There we had been, spending half the night shooting at two men and a big supply of firecrackers! Well, no use crying about it now. Hoofprints up the stream a way, where the rustlers had staked out their mounts. They rode off to the west, it looked like, after they'd had their fun.

I sat down to think about it. Almost went to sleep. I guess I would have, if about that time somebody hadn't tried to kill me.

The bullet ripped through the brush

and slammed into the soft clay wall of the creek bank. Six inches from my head, maybe. No more than that. I never heard the crack of the rifle. I pitched forward into the creek bed, falling about a foot from the water. I started to claw for my .45.

But what good was a six-gun going to do me? I hadn't heard the rifle, just the bullet. That meant that the sound of the rifle and the bullet got here about the same time and whoever was doing the bushwhacking was a long way off. What was I going to do now?

I didn't do anything. I lay there and hoped that I had fallen out of the line of fire and that the rifleman believed he had got me with that first shot. Maybe it wasn't so smart. He could move around a little and put a bullet right in my back — if the bushwhacker was cold-blooded enough to shoot what he thought was a dead man. But I couldn't think of anything better. If I tried to move he would get me. He would sure pick me off that big black gelding if I tried to make a run for it.

So I lay there and sweated. How long, I don't know. Too long, though. I got to be an old man lying there and wondering if and when another bullet was going to come crashing in. I made up my mind to quit stock detecting and take up something else, if I got out of this. The turnover was too high in this business. Almost beat to death, almost stabbed, and now bushwhacked, all in the space of two days. And what would I get out of it? A cheap burial, maybe, if that rifleman decided to finish it off. A bawling-out from my boss in Fort Worth, probably, if he didn't. The pay wasn't high enough for this sort of thing.

Still I lay there. Where was he? Who was he? Why the hell was he sniping at me? I couldn't answer any of these questions. Not now. Time dragged by like hamstrung terrapins. The sun was setting in the west. The light wasn't too good for bushwhacking purposes, but that wasn't saying it wasn't good enough. No more bullets, though.

After a long, long time I heard the faraway sound of a horse settling down to a nice easy gallop. I began to breathe again. It looked like my friend had decided that I was dead and there was no use burning up any more ammunition. The hoofbeats got fainter and faster. He seemed to be in a hurry.

I guess that was when I began to get mad. I was tired getting kicked around like a homeless pot-hound. I wanted to get my hands around somebody's throat and squeeze it until eyes popped out like wine corks.

It was a bad time for the saddle-fagged, puzzle-eyed cowhand to come riding up.

When I heard the horse I pulled my .45 and got behind some brush. I didn't know then that he was just an innocent cowhand. Maybe it was somebody else wanting to get me measured for a pine box. Well, by God, there'd be some powder burned before he got the job done! He spotted my black gelding and craned his neck around to see where the rider was. That was when I stepped out and said, 'God-dam you, if you as much as bat an eye I'll scatter your brains all over this lousy landscape.'

That froze him. He sat there popeyed and stupid-looking, not moving a muscle.

'Now who the hell are you?' I said. 'And what are you doing sniffing around this creek?'

He looked like he was about to have a bad chill. 'Christ, you about scared me blind!' he wheezed. 'Don't you know me?'

'I never saw you before.'

'Sure you did. Last night. Hell, I rode out with you from the Box-A.'

At last I pegged him. He was one of Albert's riders, just a run-of-the-mine saddle-warmer that you wouldn't ordinarily look at the second time. But I remembered seeing that face of his the night before. I took a deep breath, let it out, and then dropped my gun back in the holster.

'I'm sorry I jumped you like that,' I said. 'I guess I'm a little out of sorts.'

He grinned, but it was pretty watery. 'Hell, I know what you mean, after last night. I thought I heard some shooting, though. That's the reason I came down here to have a look.'

'Everything's all right,' I said. 'I was just nosing around.'

He scratched his chin. He'd heard some shooting and he kind of wanted to insist on it. But he decided it wasn't worth it. 'Well,' he said, 'I guess I'll get back to nursing cows, if everything's all right.'

I watched him ride off. He was a good boy. He wasn't much to look at, and he would never get into anybody's history book — but in my book he was somebody special, because he'd saved my life. I knew now why the rifleman hadn't come down to see what kind of job he had done. The cowhand scared him off.

That brought up something else. Why had I been bushwhacked in the first place?

Because I knew too much. Anyway, that was what he must have thought. But how would I know anything? We hadn't found anything in the badlands.

And there wasn't anything here on the creek . . .

Or was there?

I went back down in a hurry and started scrabbling around in the brush and dirt. The same old burnt-out fire-crackers, the same boot prints and hoof prints. No calling cards. Not even a handy horseshoe to take to a blacksmith so he could tell me where it came from. Nothing. Except a dead man.

I hadn't seen him the first time around because he was shoved under the naked roots of a cottonwood and partly covered with leaves. I wouldn't have found him this time, probably, if I hadn't slipped and grabbed at the roots for support. Some of the leaves fell away and there he was.

He was dead, all right. A rifle bullet had gone in at the right temple and out the left. Nice and clean. Not much blood. His eyes were bulged out, the way eyes will do when you get shot in the head.

I had never seen him before. He was about forty years old — the small, tight-wound type, with a smooth, oily-looking face. Probably had been hell with the ladies in his livelier days; dressed more like a gambler than a cowman. I pulled him out and rolled him around with the toe of my boot. Well, it looked like somebody had got lucky last night — one of Albert's riders, or Northern's, or Phillips'. The dead man still had a piece of punk in his hand, and I could see him now — laughing like a fool, just about to set off another string of firecrackers that those bone-headed ranchers thought were rifles, and about the time he stopped laughing and started dying. It must have been a great shock to him. His face still looked surprised.

But I still didn't know what there was about the dead man that would make somebody want to kill me before I found him. Maybe something in his pockets would tell me. I started shaking him down and found three dollars in silver in his pants pocket along with a small folding knife, a couple of broken match sticks and some lint. There was a .45 on

his hip and a little double-barreled derringer. In his vest pocket, which didn't
surprise me much. He looked like the
kind of man to carry a derringer. In his
shirt pocket there was a sack of tobacco,
son wheat-straw papers and some more
matches. Nothing there to tell me anything. The only thing to do was to load
him up and take him back to the Box-A
and see if anybody there knew him.

★   ★   ★

It was dark by the time I got back to the
ranch house. No lights in the bunkhouse
or foreman's house. Everybody was trying to catch up on their sleep, I guessed.
I rode up in front of the foreman's house
and yelled, 'Vic!'

I imagined that I heard him curse. A
lamp went up and in a minute he opened
the door. 'What the hell?' he said. 'I
thought you was dead to the world.'

'You don't know how right you almost
were,' I said. 'I found something down
on the creek. See if you can tell me what

it is.'

'On the creek?' He stood there, trying to gouge the sleep out of his mind. 'Wait a minute, until I get my boots on.'

He disappeared, and in a minute he came out again, wearing his red underwear, hat, and boots. He had a lantern in his hand. By that time I had the dead man stretched out on the ground, face up.'There he is,' I said. 'You ever see him before?' Vic Schuyler held the lantern close to the dead man's face. 'Well, I'll be goddamned,' he said softly. He moved the lantern up and down. 'Where did you say you found him?'

'Down on the creek. He was one of those birds we were playing war with last night. He must have got careless and stuck his head up and hit a rifle bullet.'

The foreman grunted. He rolled the dead man around with the toe of his boot, the same as I had done. Then he began going through the pockets. 'He didn't have anything on him except three dollars and some trash,' I said.

The foreman stood up, frowning. 'You

found somethin', all right,' he said, 'but I don't know just what's goin' to come of it. That hunk of meat you brought in used to be Kurt Basser.'

I was getting pretty groggy. The name rolled around in my mind for several seconds before it finally found the slot and went in. 'You mean the number-one suspect for the boss rustler's job? Excepting the members of the Big Three, of course.'

'He's the one.' Vic scratched his chin. 'Well, I guess I'd better get the boss woke up and see what he says to do with it.'

I meant to ask the foreman if he knew of anybody who thought he was pretty good with a long-range rifle, but I forgot it. I began to have visions of feather beds and long black hours of unconsciousness. I stumbled up the two steps to the foreman's house and started pulling off my clothes. That was the last I remembered.

6

It must have been noon the next day when I finally came out of it. Vic Schuyler was off somewhere. One of his jugs was empty and another one had been hit pretty hard. Wherever he was, he was in pretty good shape.

I went out and asked the wrangler what had happened to my dear friend, and he said the Sheriff had come out and taken the body back to town. Schuyler and Albert had gone along too.

I kind of had a hankering to ride into town too and spend some of George Albert's forty dollars on a schooner of cold beer, but there was a little matter of bushwhacking I wanted to look into first. I was just getting Dusty saddled up when the wrangler came out and began throwing leather on a speedy-looking little mare.

'Somebody else going for a ride?' I asked.

'Miss Albert,' the wrangler grunted moodily. 'She'll get herself killed some-day on this mare. No kind of a horse for a woman.'

'Why don't you rig up something a lit-tle gentler?'

He gave me a sad look. 'You ever goin' to cross a woman like that?'

I knew what he meant. Just as I was climbing on Dusty, Jane Albert came out. 'You finally wake up, Mr. Reagan?' she asked brightly.

'I got hungry,' I said, 'and nobody would serve me breakfast in bed.' I tried to get away, but I guess I'd used all my luck the day before.

'You riding south?' she asked.

'Over to see Northern and Phillips.'

'Good, I'll come along with you.'

So we rode around the barns and out of the ranch yard and over the prairie and across the creek. The sun was blaz-ing away like a farm oven at harvest time, but Jane Albert stayed as cool and beau-tiful as ever in her corduroy riding outfit with the split skirt She didn't mention the little tussle we'd had a couple of nights back. But once in a while she would turn that heavy-lidded gaze on me and I knew she was thinking about it.

We finally raised Northern's ranch house, and it was quite a place. Another one of those sprawling affairs, not quite as big as the Albert ranch house, but he was trying. There was a skeleton wing on the north side where he was adding a couple more rooms, and some workmen were laying the foundation for what was going to be the fourth fireplace.

Everything, including the outbuildings and corrals, was glistening with new paint.

'Isn't it lovely!' Jane Albert said happily.

'It's quite a place, all right,' I said. 'Does Northern have a big family?'

'Oh, no,' she said. 'He lives alone. He does now, anyway. He's proposed to me, you know.'

I smiled.

'Ran has, too, for that matter,' she said.

I said, 'When are you going to stop

117

hazing them? Or maybe you're just waiting for one to shoot the other. It would be more exciting that way, wouldn't it?'

Those blue eyes clouded as she frowned. 'You're not exactly bullet-proof yourself, Mr. Stock Detective. All I have to do is mention the other night, and you'd find out.'

That reminded me of that bushwhacker. I said, 'You haven't already got somebody gunning for me, have you?'

She laughed. 'Not yet.' Then she leaned toward me, still laughing softly. 'I don't have to tell anybody, you know. All you have to do is be nice; that's not going to hurt you.'

I wasn't so sure about that. Anyway, our little chitchat was cut short as we rode into the ranch yard and Northern's wrangler came toward us.

'Hello, Mac,' Jane Albert called. 'Is Mr. Northern here?'

'Howdy, Miss Jane,' the wrangler said. 'No ma'am, he ain't here. Think maybe he went to town.' Jane Albert turned to me. 'Well, Mr. Stock Detective, where do we go from here?'

'Are you going to follow me around the rest of the day?'

'I may,' she said sweetly. 'It depends on how long it takes me to get bored with you.'

What can you do with a girl like that? 'Well,' I said, 'we might as well go on and make the rounds of your boyfriends, then. You can show me the way to Phillips' place; I've never been there.'

She was beginning to get under my skin, and she loved it. She smiled a wide, bright smile, and we headed almost due west. We never got to the Phillips place, though. We were interrupted by a couple of old friends of mine, the two hard cases who called themselves Huck and Kramer.

We were close enough to shake hands before I knew they were even in Texas. We hit the bend in Hound Dog Creek, not far from where we'd held our sham battle, and there they were. It surprised them as much as it did me, I guess. They were just breaking out of some brush when we met head-on on the west bank of the creek.

I should have pulled my .45 and shot holes in both of them while they sat there gawking, but I didn't do it. Then the one called Kramer said something — a curse, I think — and started grabbing leather. But he wasn't very fast. He was better with knucks than he was with guns. Anyway, about that time Huck put steel to his horse and threw everything out of kilter.

I guess he was going to make a run for it, but his horse got tangled up in the brush and went down. The next thing I knew the air was full of bullets.

Jane Albert began howling and I knew we had to get out of there. There was nothing that would suit me better than a shoot-out with my old pals, but a thing like that can't be done when you've got a girl beside you. I yelled for her to get out and I would try to hold them off, but then that fiery little chestnut of hers started acting up and wouldn't go any-where but around in circles.

It was no time for anything funny. Bullets were too thick for things like that. So I kicked Dusty a good one and dived out of the saddle, grabbing Jane Albert on the way down and dragging her. We somersaulted down the bank of the creek and wound up behind a clump of willows. But willows are not very substantial things when bullets are whistling. We clawed our way up the bank to where a flood had washed up a cottonwood log some time or other, and that was as far as we were going.

My two friends were seeing to that. They were burning the air down now, and I don't know why they didn't knock us down while we were scrabbling around in the mud, unless maybe they were as excited as I was. Anyway, they missed their good chance, and now we had a fortress to make a stand behind.

I had my own .45 unlimbered by now and began banging away. Jane Albert was clawing at me and yelling, so I didn't do any good.

'Stop it, will you!' I said sharply. 'Those

boys are after my hide. They mean business.'

I shoved her away and she began to swell up like a poisoned toad. 'Stop it, yourself!' she yelled in my face. 'Those men are our riders!'

'They're what?'

'They're our own riders! They work for the Box-A!'

That jarred me. 'Well, by God, you'd better tell your father to be more careful in picking his help. This is the second time they've tried to kill me.'

'You're crazy,' she snapped. 'Why would they want to kill you? They've been stationed out on one of the line camps; they don't even know who you are.'

I said, 'I guess you're going to tell me that their shooting at us is all a mistake?'

'That's exactly what it is,' she said. 'Just watch and you'll find out.' She stood up then, before I could stop her. 'Jake!' she yelled. 'Bass! Don't shoot. It's me, Jane Albert!'

About that time a gun exploded and

a bullet snapped at the hem of her corduroy riding skirt and almost tore it off. That convinced her. Her face paled. For a minute I thought she was going to faint. I reached up and jerked her down behind the log.

'Well,' I said, 'is it still a mistake?'

Her lips were almost white. They quivered a little, but not much. 'What does it mean?' she asked hoarsely. 'Why would they want to shoot at us?'

'I don't know, and right now I'm not particularly interested. All I want to do is stop it.' I began easing my head around the end of the log to see if I could find out where they were. There was a flat, business-like report and I felt a little tug at my head. My hat went sailing down the creek bank.

Somebody had broke out a saddle gun.

They meant business, all right. On top of that, they were a lot smarter than I had figured at first. Jane Albert had called them Jake and Bass. While they were working on me with those knucks they had called each other Huck and Kramer. For hired killers, that was being pretty careful.

'What are we going to do?' Jane Albert said tightly.

'You might go through a few quick prayers,' I said, 'if you know any. Somebody's got a rifle over there. He can keep us nailed down behind this log and the other one can scoot around behind us and put bullets in our backs.'

'Do-do you really think they'll do that?'

'That's what I would do, if I were in their place.' I eased my gun around the log again to see what would happen. Sure enough, whack, whack, two bullets came smashing into the log. For a minute there was a little rain of dust and pieces of bark, then I saw a little curl of smoke drifting up from a clump of blackjack. I put two bullets into the blackjack — pretty close, I guess, because I heard some scooting and the next shot came from behind cottonwood.

Then it got quiet. I reloaded while

they thought it over. Jane Albert lay there close to the log, looking as if she might start whimpering.

'Look,' I called out suddenly, 'I don't know what you two birds have got against me, but I'm willing to settle it any way you say. Only I've got a woman with me. Why don't you boys just hold your fire for a while until she gets out of here? Then we'll go on with the war.'

Leaves rattled. The wind moaned. That was all.

'All right,' I shouted, 'you suggest something.'

'Go to hell,' one of them called nastily.

That was Kramer. Old Johnny-behind-the-brass-knucks.

'Well,' I said to Jane Albert, 'it looks like they're not going to give us anything. It's about time for one of us to get an idea before it's too late.'

She just stared at me with those wide blue eyes, scared eyes now. Huck started popping away with that saddle gun of his, and I popped back with my .45, neither of us getting anywhere. The other one, I guessed, had already pulled out and was getting into position for some back shooting.

I'd seen some icy ones in my time, but this was the first time I ever saw anybody deliberately set out to kill a woman. They couldn't have had anything against Jane Albert except for the fact that she knew they had worked on me back in New Orlando. But that was enough. One thing could lead to another, in this business. I guess they figured it was better to stop it right now, before it went any further.

So I did the only thing I could. I tried to hold Huck behind the cottonwood and prayed that Kramer would break a leg before he got behind us. I was beginning to get the range on that cottonwood. I could see bark fly when I let go with a shot. He couldn't shoot so well under conditions like that.

If it hadn't been for the girl, maybe I would have tried something crazy, like rushing the rifleman, hoping to finish him off before the other one got into position. But I couldn't very well do that now. What if I caught a bad case of bullet sickness before I could reach the cottonwood? That would leave Jane Albert in a fine spot . . . It got quiet again.

'Are you sure these two are on your father's payroll?' I asked.

She nodded stiffly. She was past talking, I guess. I didn't try to figure it out. It was a little late to work on any problem except the one that might get us out of this mess. Off to the right somewhere a twig snapped. Or I thought a twig snapped. I listened and listened and heard nothing. If it was Kramer up there, he was being pretty quiet about it. I couldn't see anything but some brush and briars and a wild plum tree. Then Huck put two more bullets into our private fortress, trying to wear it down, I guess, or cover up for Kramer.

What I did next wasn't the smartest thing in the world — but it was something. I checked my .45 and there were three rounds left. I punched out the empties and loaded it to the brim, not the usual five rounds, but six. This was no time to be worried about my gun going off in my holster. After I got it loaded I began emptying it as fast as I could, one explosion crashing on top of the other.

It was a damn fool thing to do, actually. It was shooting at ghosts. I hadn't seen anything. I wasn't even sure that I had heard anything. What was worse, I had emptied my pistol completely, and if the rifleman had been counting the shots he would have known it was empty and he could have stepped from behind his tree and finished it off.

But my luck had taken a change for the better. Maybe he had never learned to count. Anyway, he didn't take advantage of it. Somewhere in the middle of all that shooting I heard somebody howl, and I knew then I would have to play it close to the vest from here on out because I had just used up enough luck to last a year. One of those wild bullets had Kramer's name on it.

I could hear him thrashing around up there now. He groaned and cursed once or twice, and then his voice kind of trailed off. Suddenly it was quiet once more. No sound from the brush at all.

Well, that kind of changed things. It was just me and Huck now. Kramer's sins had caught up with him. I punched the empties out again and started to reload, and I guess that was when Huck finally came out of his trance and realized what had happened. Maybe he heard me ramming those empty cartridge cases out of my .45. I don't know. Maybe he was just a little crazy. Anyway, he came charging out from behind his tree, firing a snub-barreled carbine from the hip as he ran.

A man can't shoot worth a damn that way. He should have known it, and maybe he did, but he came on anyway, his face all twisted, and shooting as fast as he could jack cartridges into the chamber. Maybe he thought it was time for the lucky cards to fall on his side.

But it wasn't his lucky day. He was almost shoving that carbine down my throat by the time I got one cartridge in my .45. There was great surprise on his face when I shot him. I just stuck the pistol in front of me and pulled the trigger. I couldn't miss. He stopped as if he had run into a stone wall. His eyes sort of glassed over, he staggered, almost went down. But not quite. He was tough. They don't come like him very often.

He pulled himself together and took off in a staggering in toward the brush. He fell on his face and began scrabbling around, out of sight. He wasn't dead yet. That carbine exploded again and the bullet kicked dirt in my face and went screaming across the creek.

Tough, all right, but not tough enough to take a .45 slug in the gut and live for long. It was a matter of time now. I could sit behind my log and smoke a couple of cigarettes and by that time all his blood would have leaked out and that would be the end.

That was what I thought, anyway.

Maybe five minutes went by and then I called, 'You don't have to lay there in the weeds and die, you know.'

That saddle gun spoke again and

burned a hole in the hot afternoon.

'Why don't you give it up?' I said. 'I'll tell you what I'll do. You just give me the name of whoever hired you for this job and I'll get you the best doctor in New Orlando.'

Another bullet, just about four inches over my head this time.

'Your pal's dead, you know,' I called.

Just a curse this time. Maybe he was out of ammunition. But I didn't believe it enough to step into the open. We had another spell of silence and I noticed Jane Albert for what seemed the first time in hours. She wasn't as hard and brittle as she had been before. She had been pretty close to death — closer than she had ever been before, probably — and it had taken something out of her.

'It's all over now,' I said, 'but the waiting. One of them is dead; the other one will be dead.'

She looked at me. A little of her confidence came back, but her voice was very small. 'Hold me, Pat. Hold me tight.'

'Thanks just the same, but I'd rather

have my hands free.'

That got her out of it. Anger and hate, and maybe a little shame, started clouding those clear blue eyes of hers. 'Damn you!' she hissed. 'Damn you! Damn you!'

I grinned at her. She was beginning to be her nice sweet self again.

Now that it looked like most of the excitement was over, I could get back to wondering why so many people were so interested in seeing me dead. The rustling? More than likely. I would like to get the rifleman to answer a question or two, but I didn't know how to go about it.

'Is Jake his name?' I asked Jane Albert. 'The one that's been using that saddle gun on us.'

'Jake,' she said. 'I don't know his last name.'

'How long has he worked on the Box-A?'

'I'm not sure — about two months. When the rustling started, all the ranchers started hiring men like them . . .' The more she thought about it the madder she got. 'I hope he doesn't die!' she said tightly. 'I want to see him hang!'

'I'll bet,' I said. But I don't think she heard me. Her eyes were half-closed, and I knew that in her mind she was seeing the two killers dangling from the highest gallows, and she was enjoying it. Well, I couldn't blame her.

Quite a bit of time had gone by since we'd heard from the carbine. I managed to get my head over the log without stopping a bullet.

'This is your last chance, Jake. Do you want to tell me who hired you to kill me?'

No answer. I didn't think I was going to get one. I checked my .45 and began crawling toward the brush. After a few minutes I called back to Jane Albert.

'You might as well stand up and stretch your legs. It's all over.'

'Are — are you sure?'

I was sure. Huck — or Jake — was lying face up in the weeds, staring with wide-open eyes at some point in the sky about a million miles off . Well, he had been a tough one, and a stubborn one, too. No chance to get my answers out of him now. The ground around him was soaked and warm with blood, and flies were already beginning to swarm. I heard Jane Albert coming through the weeds, and I said, 'You'd better stay back. This isn't very pretty.'

But she came on anyway and stood looking down at the dead man, curiously, with no emotion at all except maybe a controlled anger.

I went through his pockets. Nothing there to get excited about. I went over to the plum tree to have a look at the other one. He had died the hard way, a bullet in his throat and one in his chest. The ground was all clawed up and bloody where he had thrashed around like a headless chicken. Nothing in his pockets except a brass knuck and some loose ammunition. Well, there they were, and they had given me a hard time, but I could mark them off my list now. We heard some horses then, and I walked out of the brush and saw a couple of riders coming across the flats from the west.

'Do you know them?' I called to Jane

Albert.

'Yes, they're Ran Phillips' riders. One of them is his foreman.'

The riders pushed through the brush toward Jane Albert, and one of them, a big open-faced, honest-looking sort of jasper that I took to be the foreman, said, 'Miss Albert, you all right? Was all that shootin' goin' on down here?'

'This is the place,' I said, 'and everybody's all right, except a couple of dead men over there in the weeds.'

The foreman rode over to the dead rifleman and sat there for maybe a full half-minute, staring down at the body. He said, 'This one's dead, all right. We was over to the west lookin' for strays when we heard the commotion. We got here as fast as we could, but I guess it was too late to do any good.' He looked at me. 'What was the trouble?'

'It's a long story,' I said, 'but maybe Miss Albert will tell you about it if you'll escort her back.'

That got a rise out of her, as I knew it would. 'What if I don't want to go home?'

'You'll go anyway,' I said, and surprisingly, she didn't argue about it. 'Look,' I said to the foreman, 'do you think you could have a rider and a hack of some kind get these two bodies into New Orlando? I think your boss will say it's all right. Is he at the ranch house?'

'He's in to town, I think,' the foreman said, 'but I don't think it'll be any trouble. Fred,' he said to the other rider, 'how about you getting the buckboard hitched while I see Miss Albert home?'

That seemed to settle things. Fred lit out for the west again, and Jane Albert and Phillips' foreman rode off toward the east. I settled down to another spell of waiting. After a while Fred came back with the buckboard, we loaded the bodies in the back end and headed for New Orlando.

★ ★ ★

It was around supper time when we got to town. I left Dusty with my talkative friend at the livery barn and rode down to the Star Bar in the buckboard. I figured that was where I would find Albert, and maybe Northern and Phillips, as well. But they weren't there. According to the bartender, they were in the hash house across the street.

That was where I found them, Albert and Northern and Phillips and a lean, gray-haired man that I'd never seen before. They were in a booth on the far side of the place, just sopping up the last of their steak and eggs when I came in. Northern half-stood up when he saw me and motioned for me to come over.

George Albert half-smiled as I dragged up a chair and sat down at the end of the booth. He looked worried and puzzled. Maybe he was still thinking of all those cattle he had lost.

Ran Phillips was the only one of the four that didn't make some kind of an attempt to make me feel welcome. He looked at me flatly and said, 'Well, Reagan, I guess your job in New Orlando is over.'

'I was under the impression that it was

just beginning,' I said.

Kyle Northern pushed his plate back and pulled his coffee over. 'We've finally got the man who was behind the rustling,' he said.

I supposed I must have looked surprised. I was surprised. 'Well,' I managed, 'that's fine. Who is he?'

'Kurt Basser,' George Albert said.

A waitress came up and sold the other four some apple pie while I thought it over. Then George Albert remembered himself and introduced the gray-haired man who was sitting with him as the Sheriff of Orlando County. Now that I got a closer look at him I saw that his eyes were as gray as his hair. Even his face had a gray, thoughtful look. His name was Jim Devers.

'That's the way it looks, Reagan,' the Sheriff said, digging into his pie. 'When we got Basser's body into town we found that he had a money belt on him and two thousand dollars in government greenbacks. The thing that nailed it down, though, was a tally he kept of the transaction. Two hundred head of cattle at twelve and a half dollars a head — at prices like that they couldn't have been anything but stolen cattle. Of course, the ranchers themselves can't sell their stock to the Indian reservations for the kind of money they would get in Kansas, but then, they don't have the long trail drive to make either. About twenty-five dollars a head, isn't that what they usually bring, Albert?'

George Albert nodded. 'That's what my last herd brought.'

'Well,' the Sheriff said, 'half of that would be about what a crooked Agency buyer would pay for stolen cattle. The other half he could pocket, and on the books it would show the cattle bought at full prices.'

'Just to get things straight,' I said, 'Basser didn't have two hundred head of cattle himself, did he? In case he might want to sell them at half-price for some reason?'

Kyle Northern laughed. 'Basser didn't even have twenty head of cattle. All he

139

had was a little cockle-bur outfit that would do good to support a dozen head of goats.'

'That seems to put Basser in a bad light, all right,' I said. 'Here's something else, though. If my arithmetic is right, there's five hundred dollars missing from the money belt. Two hundred cows at twelve and a half a throw comes to twenty-five hundred, doesn't it?'

'We thought of that,' Ran Phillips said coolly, in that Old Virginia Family voice of his. 'He could easily have lost that five hundred in a poker game. He was a gambler, you know.'

Everybody nodded in agreement, including the Sheriff.

'Yes,' George Albert said. 'I can't say that I had Basser figured for the boss rustler job — I didn't think he was that smart — but it looks like I was wrong. The trouble, I guess, is over.'

More nods, and everybody had another round of coffee.

'Well, by God,' I said, 'I wish somebody would pass the word around, if the trouble's over. I've been bushwhacked, slugged, gun-whipped, kicked and ambushed. The last unpleasantness happened not more than two hours ago. Two of your own men tried to put bullets in me, Albert — in your daughter too, for that matter. Remember the two hard boys I told you about? The ones crazy about brass knucks? They were the ones.'

They all stopped chewing. George Albert was the first to get his mouth to working again. 'My daughter! Do you mean Jane?'

'She's the one. I decided to make the rounds and see if I could find somebody who knew something about a long-range rifle, and she came along.'

'A long-range rifle?' Sheriff Jim Devers said.

'Yesterday somebody tried to kill me with one,' I said. 'Just before I uncovered Basser's body in the creek. By the way, do you know of any guns like that?'

'A 30–30?'

'At least. Maybe more.'

The Sheriff frowned. 'There are a lot

of 30-30's around. Got one myself.'

But Albert didn't give a damn about that now. He was already half out of his seat when I waved him down again. 'Your daughter's all right.' I said. 'Phillips' foreman came up after the shooting was over and I had him take her back to the Box-A.'

Albert settled down again, but the thing had shaken him. He took a clean handkerchief from his breast pocket and dirtied it by wiping his damp hands. 'I can't believe it,' he said shakily. 'Not two of my own men?'

'Ask your daughter,' I said.

'They — they would have killed her?'

'Not that they had anything against her,' I said. 'Just because she was with me.'

George Albert looked like a man who was going to keep his daughter away from stock detectives from now on. He was going to try, anyway. Northern and Phillips still looked a little dazed by it all.

'These men,' Ran Phillips said, 'where are they now?'

'They're outside in one of your buck-boards.'

They all sat there looking as if they didn't believe me. Finally the Sheriff wiped his mouth, put a silver dollar on the table, and got up. 'I guess there wouldn't be any use asking them any questions, would there?'

'They're pretty dead,' I said.

Very deliberately, everybody wiped their mouths, put silver dollars on the table, and began to file out. Other customers began doing the same thing. When the Sheriff got that look, I guess they knew that something was up. I fell in beside George Albert. It looked like a parade by the time we got out to the buckboard.

It was just beginning to get dark and there weren't many people on the streets, but what few there were had ganged around the buckboard, looking at the dead men. Vic Schuyler was there too, his face a little redder than usual, so I guessed that he had been sampling some of that corn whiskey that he didn't like.

He looked unhappy.

'I thought you was going to call me when you caught up with these birds,' he said.

'It happened kind of fast,' I said. 'Not that I wouldn't have appreciated your company.'

Vic Schuyler grinned suddenly, and the Sheriff began scattering the crowd. 'All right, there's no use making a circus out of this. Let's get this buckboard around to the funeral parlor and we can lay them out and do things right.'

The driver whipped the horses up and the buckboard lurched up the street, with most of the crowd trailing along behind like flies following a butcher's wagon.

'You coming, Reagan?' Albert asked.

'Not now,' I said. 'I think I'll wash up and get some supper. If you learn anything, I'll be over at the eating house.'

The buckboard and the crowd passed around a corner and out of sight, and Vic Schuyler and I stood in the dusty street and watched night come down on New Orlando. I discovered that I was very tired, and very sick of New Orlando. I ought to see about getting a job in some quiet little place where nothing ever happened. I felt dirty, and I knew that the feeling wouldn't go with washing. But I tried it, anyway. I went around to the back of the Star Bar where there was a pump, took off my shirt and scrubbed myself down. I combed my hair with my fingers, beat some of the dust from my clothes, went back in the bar and had four straight shots with Vic Schuyler. I felt better. Not good, but better.

I said, 'Tell me about my friends in the buckboard. Did you know them very well?'

'Hell,' Vic Schuyler said, 'I didn't know them at all. The boss must have hired them while I was gone and sent them out to ride the line.'

'They were in town,' I said, 'a couple of nights ago, the night I rode into this place.'

Schuyler shrugged. 'Line riders can do anything. There's nobody there to keep an eye on them.' He frowned. 'Brass knucks!' The foreman never would get over that one, I guessed.

We finished our drinks and went over to the eating house and ordered the house special, steak and eggs. As we were sopping up the gravy with soggy biscuits, and getting ready for the coffee, the Sheriff came through the door and back to our booth. 'Well, Reagan,' he said, 'this is your lucky day.'

I looked at him. 'You could have fooled me. How come?'

'It turns out there's a reward for your two dead friends. I guess you get it.'

7

Sheriff Jim Devers had an office down at the end of the block, a little whacked-up affair of white-washed plank, and alongside the office there was a sturdy little log jail.

We went into the office, me, Vic Schuyler, and the Sheriff. Vic and I pulled up leather-bottomed chairs while the Sheriff got behind a plank desk. 'Here they are,' he said, riffling through a batch of U.S. Government dodgers that he had collected over the years in his business. He selected a couple and shoved them across the desk. Sure enough, they were my friends, all right. They were the usual dodgers that county sheriffs get as a matter of routine, complete with an artist's drawing of the wanted men. At the top, in big black letters, was $500.00 REWARD, DEAD OR ALIVE.

I couldn't think of anything to say right then. It was nice to think that one of these days I'd be getting a government check for five hundred dollars, but I'd liked to have earned it some other way. Being forced to kill was one thing, but getting paid for it set a little heavy on my stomach.

'Seems they killed a U.S. Marshal down on the Border,' Jim Devers said. 'That's how come the reward. Usually I don't pay much attention to these dodgers, because gunmen like that almost never show up in New Orlando. But after I got a look at those jaspers in the buckboard I got to wondering. Sure enough, when I came back and started going through the files, there they were.'

Vic Schuyler sat back and laughed. 'Well, by God, you fell into a bucket of it that time and came out smellin' like roses.'

I said, 'That reward goes to you, Sheriff. You're the one that spotted them . . .'

But he waved me down.

'Well, half of it anyway.'

But the Sheriff wasn't having any.

I didn't feel much like celebrating, but

I said, 'Anyway, we can have a round of drinks.'

'That's the way to talk!' Vic Schuyler said.

So we went back to the Star Bar where the evening's entertainment was just getting under way. A fish-eyed young man thumped tinny music out of a battered piano that looked like it had been dragged from St. Louis to Abilene, and then kicked around from one deadfall to another until it finally found its way across the desert and into New Orlando. There was a pretty good crowd, and more drifting in all the time, mostly ranchers and cowhands, and now and then a sharpshooter waiting for somebody to get too drunk to watch his money. There were maybe a half-dozen saloon girls with iron-hard smiles and laughter that grated on your nerves like a bone saw until you'd had a few drinks of the house poison, and then they all began to look like the Queen of Sheba, or better. We elbowed our way to the bar and the bartender brought the bottle out.

We all had a drink and I said, 'Did you make anything out of the dead men?'

The Sheriff shook his head. 'All I know about them is what I read in the dodgers.'

'Do you peg them as part of the rustling gang? That would be a pretty setup, if they could swing it, planting a few of their men around on different ranches.'

Jim Devers shrugged. 'Might be. More than likely, though, they just wanted a place to hide from the government marshals, so they figured a place like New Orlando would be about the thing. I guess they were right, as far as that goes. It was just an accident that we got them.'

'Not quite,' I said. 'Remember they damn near beat my brains out the first time I laid eyes on them.'

'That's right,' the Sheriff said thoughtfully. 'You sure you never run into them before? Maybe in line with your work?'

'Not that I remember.'

We all had another drink. Vic Schuyler had two.

'Maybe we ought to go back to the

funeral parlor,' the Sheriff said after a while. 'They ought to be all prettied up by now. With their faces washed and shaved, maybe they'll look different.'

I doubted it but there wasn't much to lose by having another look at them. 'Well, all right. Coming, Vic?'

'I think I'll stay and have a few more,' the foreman said. So we left him at the bar and met Kyle Northern just as we were pushing through the bat wings.

'Anything doing at the funeral parlor?' I asked.

'Just talk,' Northern said. 'I've had enough for one day. Come on back and I'll buy a round of drinks.'

'No, thanks,' I said. 'The Sheriff thinks we ought to go over and nose around once more.'

We went up the plankwalk and Northern was swallowed up in the noise and smoke and confusion of the Star Bar.

* * *

The Palmer Funeral Parlor was just another two-story frame house, about a block west of Main Street, behind a dry-goods store and a harness shop. There was a rock walk up to the front porch, and a few rose bushes in the front yard. There was a big frosted glass pane in the front door and some black lettering that said Ferguson Funeral Parlor. Ferguson had died a while back, the Sheriff said, with lung fever. Palmer hadn't got around to changing the lettering yet.

It didn't make much difference. It was the only funeral parlor in town, but at the rate things were going Palmer might have to spread out a little. Three customers in one day was pretty good for a town the size of New Orlando.

The Sheriff opened the door and we walked into the front room, which was kind of a reception room, I guess. There were no bodies. The Boor was spongy with red-plush carpeting. A couple of heavy chairs and a couch stood against the walls. American Rag on a staff drooped limply in one of the darker corners of the room.

George Albert and Ran Phillips and a nervous little man, that I took to be the undertaker, came out of one of the back rooms as we came into the front room. Albert and Phillips were putting their hats on, as if they were getting ready to leave.

Albert said, 'You coming back out to the Box-A, Reagan?'

'Not right now,' I said. 'I want to have another look at my two friends.'

'Well,' the Box-A owner said heavily, 'I think I've seen enough. I'm going on home, Reagan. You can come on out with Vic if you want to.'

I said that would be fine, and we all said good night, and Albert and Phillips went out to the front porch.

'You going to stay in town for a while, Ran?' I heard Albert say.

'No,' Phillips said, 'I'm going home too.'

Then the front door closed and the Sheriff and I were alone with the undertaker.

Mr. Palmer was of no particular age — somewhere between forty and sixty. He had a glossy, round little head, as naked of hair as the palm of your hand. His eyes were pale and watery and kind of red.

'Palmer,' Jim Devers said, 'this here is Mr. Reagan. He's a stock detective, if you haven't heard. We want to have a look around the back room. Have you got them prettied up yet?'

'Oh, yes,' Palmer said in a high, twittery voice. 'That is, I have them shaved. Of course, I haven't had time to do anything else. So many people . . . ' His voice trailed off.

'That's all right,' the Sheriff said. 'We won't be long.'

We went through a door and into another room, and there they were, laid out on some planks across sawhorses, as stiff as new saddles. A coal-oil lamp on a high mantel cast a sickly light on their yellow faces. The Sheriff said, 'You can't very well call them beauties, even after the shave.' He went over and poked one of them in the ribs just to make sure that he was good and dead. 'Well, Reagan, what do you say?'

'I never saw them before. With whiskers or without.'

'It was just an idea.' The Sheriff shrugged. 'But not worth a damn, it looks like. What have you got over here, Palmer?' He motioned at another sawhorse contraption with a figure on it covered with a white sheet.

The undertaker wrung his hands. 'That's Mr. Basser,' he said sadly. 'Poor Mr. Basser.'

'Poor Mr. Basser, hell!' the Sheriff snarled. 'The sonofabitch was stealing the ranchers blind. Well, we don't want to miss anything. Let's have a look at him too.'

'Oh, no!' Mr. Palmer gasped.

The Sheriff frowned. 'What's the matter?'

'Well . . . I . . . ' The undertaker blinked his eyes several times and wrung his hands. 'Well, it just isn't decent!'

'Decent, hell!' the Sheriff said. 'It's

your job, isn't it, to fix dead folks up pretty so people can stand to look at them?' He grabbed one corner of the sheet, gave it a jerk.

'Ha, ha!' the Sheriff laughed. 'Look at him. Looks silly as hell, don't he, without his boots on?' Not very gently put, but the Sheriff was right. A man looks pretty silly all dressed and brushed and shaved, but without his boots. With a pair of naked, ugly white feet sticking up toward the moon.

'Where the hell is his boots?' the Sheriff said. 'He may be a rustler, but a man ought to be buried with his boots on, rustler or not. Where are they?'

Mr. Palmer looked as if somebody was slowly working a knife between his ribs. His bald head glistened. He looked worried as hell. The situation didn't call for that much worry.

That was when I began to get an idea. A dead man without boots. It didn't mean a thing, in itself, but one thing led to another and after a while I began to wonder:

Say a man has a little money he doesn't know what to do with. Say five hundred dollars. Or say he has something he wants to hide. Something not very big — paper, probably. Where would he put it? In his boot. That's where a canny gambler like Kurt Basser would put it.

Five hundred dollars wasn't so big if you had it in hundred-dollar bills. An Indian agent would pay off that way. The two thousand dollars didn't count — that belonged to somebody else, so he wore it in a money belt.

Not much of an idea maybe, but it was mine.

All right, say Basser had something in his boot. I didn't find it, the Sheriff didn't find it, and neither did George Albert or Vic Schuyler. We were too busy being smart. But somebody not so smart — say an undertaker — that would probably be the first thing he would do. Take the boots off. A man can't make much of a living undertaking for the county. What's wrong in picking up a few extra dollars if somebody else doesn't run across it first? Nothing, I guess. Mr. Palmer looked like a man who wasn't too particular where a dollar came from. Something like that was the way my mind was running. Meanwhile the Sheriff was still yelling that Basser ought to have some boots on.

'Well, by God . . . ' the Sheriff said. 'Oh, here they are.'

He found them behind some zinc tubs in the corner of the room. He lifted them, looked at them. He frowned.

'Well, what the hell?' he said. 'They're cut all to pieces!' He turned to Palmer. 'What's going on here, anyway? You waited until he got stiff and then cut the boots off his feet. What's the idea of a thing like that?'

I said, 'I've got an idea, Sheriff , if you want to hear about it.'

He turned on me. 'All right, what is it?'

'Well, in the first place, Mr. Palmer's been pretty busy today. What with Albert and Northern and Phillips bothering him all day, he hasn't had much time to take care of his undertaking. When he finally got around to Basser, he was already stiff. So instead of taking his boots off, he had to cut them off.'

'But why did he take them off in the first place? He didn't take the other clothes off.'

Then he began to get it. He walked over to the undertaker and said in a quiet, businesslike voice, 'All right, Palmer, what did you find in those boots?'

The undertaker began to shake. He tried to get a hold of himself, but the effort left him weak. His mouth began to work — but we never heard what he was going to say. An explosion jarred the room. The noise went around and around the naked walls, and it looked like the Ferguson Funeral Parlor was going to have a change of hands again. Mr. Palmer was dead.

He kind of jerked, and half of his head flew off. A .45 bullet, probably. The Sheriff and I stood there frozen as he went down. He half-turned and began to melt to the floor, like a wax candle on a hot day. It seemed to take him a week to fall, but I don't suppose it was more than a second or two. He hit the floor finally, and we stood there staring at him for another second or two, then we came out of it.

'Damnation!' the Sheriff bellowed.

We crowded out the back door of the place and burst into an alleyway that was as dark as the inside of a tar barrel. I stumbled over something — a rock, I think — and went down. But the Sheriff went plunging on into the blackness, shouting like a drunken mule skinner. My .45 was out, but I couldn't see anything to shoot at. If I shot down the alleyway, I would probably hit the Sheriff. I rested on one knee and tried to hear something. No sound but the distant, confused noise coming from the Star Bar, and, of course, the racket the Sheriff was making. I got up and started after him.

We got down to where the cross street entered into Main Street, and still no sign of the killer. 'Hell's fire!' the Sheriff said, and I knew the thought had hit him the same time it hit me. Probably the killer hadn't run at all. He had just laid low and waited for us to charge out like a couple of wall-eyed coots. We started back for the funeral parlor at a dead run and heard a horse break into a gallop at the far end of the street.

'That's him!' the Sheriff yelled. 'Get a horse! Any horse!'

So we headed back for Main Street again. I jerked a dappled gray away from the hitching rack and put the iron to him. The gray wasn't used to strange hombres crawling on top of him that way and raking his ribs with spur rowels. He wanted to pitch a little. We went around in circles, and finally got straightened out toward the far end of Main Street. By that time the Sheriff had found himself a horse too, and we fogged it like a pair of Apaches.

'There he is!' the Sheriff yelled. 'I see him.'

I saw him, too. I saw the horse, that is. It was a big black horse, and he was

161

standing by the side of the road as we reined up, nibbling at some dry grass along the bar ditch.

The saddle was empty. I reached over and felt of the leather. It was cold. There hadn't been a rider in that saddle for at least a couple of hours.

Sheriff Jim Devers groaned. It was a long, drawn-out groan, full of misery and frustration. I knew how he felt. The horse had been hitched somewhere down at the end of the street; the killer came by, unhitched him, gave him a good swat across the rump, and we thought it was our man making a run for it.

The Sheriff was doing some serious cussing now, very quietly and earnestly. If I hadn't understood English, I might have thought that he was a father trying to tell his young son how dangerous it was to play with loaded guns. After a while he stopped cussing and said, 'Reagan, we're a pair of damn fools! He didn't come out of town this way. We know that, now. Let's get back down the street and see if anybody saw him leave that way. If that doesn't work, we'll get out a posse and scour the country.'

'Who're you going to look for?' I asked.

He rubbed his face. He seemed almost ready to cry. 'Hell, I don't know.'

'Well, you go see what you can find out,' I said. 'I'll go back to the funeral parlor and see if the killer left a calling card.'

Jim Devers hung steel in his horse again and spurted up the street toward the Star Bar. I galloped the gray back around to the funeral parlor.

I came in the same way I had left the place, through the back door. Mr. Palmer was still dead. His head — what was left of it — lay in a puddle of bloody slush. But he wasn't in the same position that I had last seen him. He looked as if he had been rolled around quite a bit. His pockets had all been emptied and turned inside out. A pale, blonde-haired girl who could have passed for a stone statue stood in the center of the room. She was Jane Albert.

I think I groaned. 'What the hell are

you doing here?'

Her eyes shifted just the slightest little bit. Her mouth moved. A voice of a sort came out. 'I — I heard a shot. I — came in.'

'You heard it all the way from the Box-A, I guess.'

'I was in the other room. The front room. I just came in.'

'So you heard the shot, came in here, saw the dead man and decided to go through his pockets. What did you think you'd find?'

'No — that wasn't the way it happened.' She swayed just a little. 'I just came into the other room. I heard voices — yours was one of them. Then the shot. I heard someone rush out of this room. I was afraid, I suppose — I didn't come in right away. But after a while I did. A man was going through Mr. Palmer's pockets.'

'Who was going through Mr. Palmer's pockets?'

'I don't know. Whoever it was, he had blown the lamp out. It was dark and I couldn't tell who he was.

'I heard myself groan again. 'Look,' I said, 'you'd better go somewhere and sit down and think up something better.'

I went outside again and had a look around. Sure enough, the soft dirt under the back room window was scuffed up. That's where the killer had stood to do his work. I struck a match and searched the ground, but there wasn't even a decent boot print to work on. Just a lot of scuffed-up dirt, as if the prints had been deliberately covered.

I went back into the room and Jane Albert was still standing there. 'Go in the other room and sit down,' I said.

She turned and went out of the room like a sleepwalker. Palmer's stuff was scattered all over the floor around him, so I got down on my knees and began to go through it. There was about three dollars in silver scattered around, a heavy turnip watch that looked like gold, a heavy chain that also looked like gold but was beginning to turn green in places. Dangling from the chain there was a lead .45 slug — one he had probably taken out of a customer at one time or another. A little penknife for paring his fingernails — silver, maybe. A piece of string that he had saved to tie something up with. That was all. Whatever it was that the killer had been hunting, he must have found.

I went into the other room, sat on the plush sofa and studied Jane Albert. 'So you didn't see who it was,' I said, taking up our conversation where we'd left off.

She shook her head.

'You said the lamp was out. It was burning when I came in.'

She held out a hand, opened it, and there lay a burnt match stick.

'When did you start carrying matches?'

'I haven't. The lamp was out when I came into the room and saw the man bending over Mr. Palmer. He ran out of the room, then I came in here and got a match to light the lamp with.' She pointed at a little table by the fireplace. There was a little demitasse cup full of red-headed lucifers.

I got up and walked over to the table and kicked it.

I went into the dark room again and looked around. Nothing had changed.

In the front room again, I said, 'Let's get back to my first question. What are you doing here, anyway? After that fracas this afternoon I thought you'd be satisfied for a while.'

Some of the dumbness and shock was beginning to go out of her eyes now. She frowned. 'I go where I please.' She stood up. 'Don't forget that, Mr. Stock Detective. But if you must know, Marcia and I came to town because Marcia wanted to see the dressmaker. The liveryman told us that father was at the funeral parlor, so I came up here to meet him.'

I couldn't find anything wrong with that. If a man's wife and daughter wanted to meet him in town, there was no law against it. 'Your father headed home some time ago,' I said. 'Didn't you meet him coming in?'

She shook her head. 'He must have changed his mind. Anyway, we left word with the liveryman to tell him we were in town.'

That seemed to he that. I rolled a cigarette, fired it, and sat back to wait for something to happen.

It didn't take long. I heard the crowd as they rounded the corner from Main Street, and pretty soon Albert and Phillips and Northern and Vic Schuyler came tramping up on the front porch and into the room, the Sheriff leading the way. It seemed that everybody had changed their minds about going home.

'You still here, Reagan?' the Sheriff asked. 'What did you find out?'

'The killer went through Palmer's pockets and found what he wanted before he got away. What about you?'

'Nothing,' Jim Devers said bitterly. 'I got my deputies out with a posse. But they won't find anything. It's as dark as a cellar in hell out there — excuse me, Miss Albert, I didn't see you there.'

Jane Albert smiled faintly, and George Albert said, 'Jane, what are you doing here?'

The rest of us went back to the undertaker's workroom. We all stood around and looked at Palmer as if we had never seen a dead man before.

'Joseph and Mary!' Vic Schuyler said softly. 'He sure as hell got messed up!'

'But why?' Kyle Northern said. 'Why would anybody want to murder old man Palmer?'

'He was just about to tell us what he found in Kurt Basser's boots,' the Sheriff said. 'Something we overlooked.'

'Money?' Ran Phillips said, looking at me.

I shrugged. 'Maybe. There's a chance that Palmer might have lifted the five hundred dollars missing from Basser's money belt. I think it's a good bet that he did.'

'Then maybe one of the small ranchers did it,' Phillips said. 'Basser was their friend, you know.'

We didn't like it much, but we couldn't think of anything any better. I looked at Sheriff Jim Devers. 'You want to get another posse together and see what we can find?'

'It wouldn't be any use,' he said heavily. 'We'll wait until it gets light and then try it.'

Pretty soon they all filed out again but me and the Sheriff. 'I'll see you at the saloon,' Vic Schuyler said, 'if you want me.'

'What do you think?' I said to the Sheriff.

'It's pretty clear that somebody didn't want Palmer to tell what he'd found. That's the reason he got killed. It's the reason somebody tried to bushwhack you, too, when you found Basser's body. The boss rustler did that, probably. Or hired somebody to do it. Anyway, it all ties in with the rustling.'

'It would seem that way,' I said. 'But how about the two hard cases over there on the slab?'

Jim Devers looked at them thoughtfully as they got deader and deader. 'Maybe,' he said, in a way that didn't mean much of anything.

'By the way, this crowd you brought

back with you — what were they doing when you found them?' I asked.

'Vic Schuyler and Kyle Northern were having drinks together in the Star Bar,' he said, not quite sure of what I was getting at. 'Albert was down the street in a feed store, buying some grain for his saddle stock. Phillips was in the barber shop getting a haircut.' Those gray eyes began to narrow down, like those of a man sighting carefully over the barrel of a rifle. 'Why?'

'No reason in particular. I just got to wondering about something.'

His face got stern. 'Look, Reagan, New Orlando is a lot like any other place. We got good people, bad people, poor people, rich people. Good people go bad sometime, and they have to pay for it. Bad people get worse, and you can jump on them all you want to. Poor people you can kick around just for the hell of it. The rich ones — that's something else.'

'Are you trying to tell me not to go around saying that maybe some rich people have got their fingers in the rustling pie?'

'I'm just saying that there are three big families around New Orlando. Our whole society, such as it is, is built on them. A man stays healthier dealing around outfits like that.'

For a minute we stood there looking at each other. 'But I know what you mean,' he said. 'I've been doin' some wonderin' too.'

8

I didn't go back to the Box-A that night. After leaving the Sheriff at his office, I went down to the Star Bar to have a drink with Vic Schuyler, but the foreman wasn't there. I thought maybe I'd find him at one of the other poison factories, so I went out to have a look.

I found him, but not in a saloon. He was with Marcia Albert when I saw him, carrying a big tissue-wrapped bundle that I guessed was a dress.

'Well,' I said, 'good evening, Mrs. Albert.' And we smiled at each other just like a pair of old friends. 'Vic,' I said, 'I've been looking for you.' And the foreman's face got red in embarrassment.

Marcia Albert said, 'Vic was good enough to meet me at the dressmaker's and carry my bundle for me.'

'Vic's a handy man,' I said. But she didn't get it. Neither did the foreman. He was too busy blushing, like a schoolboy carrying his girl's books home for the first time. Luckily, George Albert came up about that time, before I kept talking and got myself into trouble.

'Marcia,' he said, 'I didn't know you and Jane were coming to town. Jane's with the buggy; I've had it brought out of the livery barn. Are you ready to go?'

Marcia Albert said she was ready to go, and she asked Vic if he minded carrying the bundle just a little farther, to the buggy. Vic didn't mind at all. He would have carried it clear to California if she had asked him to. All Marcia had to do was say the word. But Marcia would never say the word because she would never know.

I watched them as they trailed down the street toward the buggy. 'Poor Vic,' I thought. I went back to the Star Bar and got myself a bottle and took it over to a table and tried to think.

There were lots of things to think about. There was pretty, blonde-haired, blue-eyed Jane Albert, for instance. I didn't want anything to do with her. And there was a beautiful dark-haired girl who had somehow married a big rancher in spite of the fact that she had been just another fancy girl not so long ago. Throw in the husband, and a couple of young ranchers — one with family and one just ambitious — and you had quite a mixture. To say nothing of the rustlers. And three dead men. Five, if you wanted to count the two I'd seen hanging.

I had a drink.

Also, just to make things more interesting, we had a foreman who was in love with his boss's wife. Who else was there, still alive? There was the Sheriff. Jim Devers was a pretty normal sort of gent, as far as I could see. That in itself was enough to make him unusual in New Orlando.

I had some more drinks.

That bushwhacker, I'd like to get my hands on that one. Taking pot shots at a man's back. My friends Huck and Kramer — they hadn't been that way. At least they could look a man in the eye while they killed him.

It all tied up with the rustling, Jim Devers said. If it did, I ought to be doing something about it. I had a job, the last I heard, with the Cattlemen's Association.

My bottle was empty. My head was light.

Business went on as usual. Huck and Kramer lay dead in the funeral parlor, along with Kurt Basser, and lately the undertaker himself, but that didn't disturb the saloon trade. Somebody gave the piano player another beer and he started . . .

> *Dearest love, do you remember*
> *When we last did meet,*
> *How you told me that you loved me*
> *Kneeling at my feet?*

It was an old Civil War song, almost as bad as 'The Vacant Chair' or 'Do Not Grieve for Thy Dear Mother,' that somehow, in spite of its sickening sentimentality, had managed to stay fairly popular in Texas — especially around midnight, in saloons like the Star Bar.

One of the saloon girls, with a wine glass clutched in one hand, leaned on the piano and began . . .

> *Weeping, sad and lonely,*
> *Hopes and fears how vain!*
> *When this cruel war is over,*
> *Praying that we meet again.*

That made up my mind for me. I went to the bar and got another bottle. When I came back to the table I had company. 'Well,' I said, 'you boys just never quite make it, do you? You say you're going home, but you never do.'

Ran Phillips looked at me with a pair of the coolest eyes I ever saw. None of that genial good fellowship now, that he displayed whenever he was around the Albert family. He was sitting on the far side of the table, very stiff and straight, with his back to the wall.

He didn't say anything, so I dropped into the chair that I'd already warmed. 'Have a drink?'

'No, thank you,' he said.

So I had one. The saloon girl finished 'Weeping, Sad and Lonely.' The piano player struck up 'The Bonnie Blue Flag.'

'You're not going to the Box-A tonight?' Phillips asked.

'No,' I said.

'Why not?'

'Because I felt like having a drink, and I was beginning to get sick of the Box-A, anyway. Now what is it you want to talk about? You don't look like a man who just dropped in to make polite conversation.'

He winced a little, but not much. 'All right,' he said, 'I have got something to talk about, but I want to ask some more questions first.'

I shrugged.

'Do you mind telling me how much money you make as an Association man?'

My eyebrows must have gone up a little at that. 'You don't aim to go into the stock detective business, do you?' He just looked at me. 'Well, all right. I get two dollars a day and furnish my own horse. I'll tell you beforehand, you'd make more money by taking a trail-driving job.'

'That's seven hundred and thirty dollars a year, isn't it?' he asked.

'I guess so, but I never saw that much money all in one piece.'

'How would you like to have a thousand dollars? All in one piece, as you say?'

He said it in that calm, well-turned voice of his. I tried to picture a thousand dollars in my mind. Have it changed into silver dollars, put them all on top of each other, and you'd have a stack of money as high as a man's head, probably. That was a lot of money.

I studied Ran Phillips to see if he was joking. He wasn't.

'How many people would I have to kill?' I said finally.

He smiled a quiet little smile that didn't quite reach his eyes. 'All you have to do,' he said, 'is leave New Orlando. And not come back.'

'Well,' I said, 'it's been a nice chat. Even if you don't drink.'

'You won't take it?'

'I've got a job,' I said. 'It's not much, as jobs go, but it's the only one I have. Besides, I wouldn't know what to do with a thousand dollars if I had it. Now can I ask a question?'

He didn't say anything.

'I'm curious to know why so many different people don't want me around. Here I come riding into New Orlando and the first thing happens, a pair of hired gun-slingers try to kill me. Then I almost get knifed — but that's another story. Then bushwhacked. Now you come along and try to buy me for a thousand dollars. Why?'

He just sat there.

'I could make some guesses,' I said. 'Would you like to hear them?'

Silence.

'All right. First, there's an idea floating around that a rancher may have a hand in the rustling. Maybe one of the big ones. This rancher, so the story goes, isn't satisfied with his lot and wants to ease the others out and grab off all the water rights along the creek. How does that sound to you?'

He came out of his shell long enough to say, 'And then what?'

'Next, we have to find some reasons. Take you, for instance. I hear you and the bankers don't get along so well. You have to have money or you're going to lose the ranch, and that would be a hard blow to the Phillips' name, wouldn't it? Of course, I don't know the details yet, but we can put a few things together. Now you offer me money to get out of town, when you aren't supposed to have any money.'

His face got a little pale and his mouth tightened around the edges, but he managed to keep his voice calm. 'Look here, Reagan, are you accusing me of stealing cattle?'

'Not yet. I'm just guessing.'

'Guess something else. Sure, I'm short of money, but not so short that I can't raise a thousand dollars. And I'm not the only one who would have something to gain. How about Kyle Northern? He started with a cocklebur spread and built it into one of the biggest ranches in this part of Texas. Do you think an ambitious man like that would stop at anything, if he saw a chance to grow bigger?'

I sat back and laughed.

'What's the matter?'

'You and Northern. The thing that puzzles me is why you haven't killed each other before now. The second time I saw Northern he accused you of being the man behind the rustling.'

He stared at me in grim, determined silence.

'But this isn't answering my question,' I said. 'Why do you want me out of New Orlando? It wouldn't have anything to do with that killing tonight, would it? The undertaker, I mean. Somebody wanted something the undertaker took off of Kurt Basser, and I guess he got it, whoever he was.'

Ran Phillips said tightly, 'Don't push me too far.'

But I wasn't listening. 'And again,' I said, thinking out loud, 'maybe it wasn't that at all. That damned Jane Albert. Did that little she-wolf . . . ?'

That was as far as I got. Ran Phillips pushed his chair back, stood up very slowly. Then he leaned across the table and hit me right between the eyes.

It wasn't much of a punch, but I wasn't ready for it. Any kind of a punch can hurt if you're not ready. He hit me and I went over backward and hit the floor with the back of my head. The table got turned over somehow, and I got mixed up in some saloon furniture. It took a while to get straightened out and get on my feet again. That whiskey had done something to my co-ordination.

As soon as I got up, he caught me behind the jaw with a looping right. I went back over some tables and chairs. The saloon girls started to scream, and the men were yelling to get back and give us room. I didn't go to the floor that time, but Phillips was right on top of me, throwing fists from every angle. I rode out the storm somehow. I was groggy, and my head hurt, and I had a feeling that I never should have gone to the bar for that second bottle, but after the first flurry things began to swing the other way. Phillips weighed about a hundred and sixty — that give me thirty pounds on him.

I finally got a fist in his middle and he grunted. He got in close and jerked his knee up to get it in my groin. I stepped back and hammered the side of his neck with the edge of my arm. His face got green. He began to go down. As he went down, my knee came up to meet his chin. He could have been a side of beef on a butcher's block for all the fuss he made after that.

It didn't take long for the Sheriff to get out of his office to see what was going on. He came through the bat wings with a sawed-off shotgun in his hands, scattering customers like a rat in a chicken house. He planted himself in front of me and glared. 'Now what the hell are you up to? Can't you keep out of trouble for a little while?'

'It doesn't look like it,' I said. I could

hardly talk, I was so winded.

He rolled Phillips over and looked at him. 'Good God, did you have to pick on a Phillips? What's the matter, couldn't you find Northern and Albert anywhere?' He turned his head and called over his shoulder. 'Bring some water, somebody!'

The bartender came over with a glass of water and the Sheriff threw it in Phillips' face. His eyes fluttered. The Sheriff got his arm around him and helped him sit up. 'How do you feel, Mr. Phillips?'

'I'm — I'm all right.' He rubbed his chin. My knee was going to be sore in the morning, but not as sore as Ran Phillips' chin.

'You need some help, Mr. Phillips?'

'No-no, I'm all right. Just let me out of here.'

He got to his feet with the Sheriff's help. He held onto a table for a while, breathing deeply. He started for the front door like a drugged man wading through clay mud. He went out and the night swallowed him.

Sheriff Jim Devers turned on me. 'All right, you, march.'

'Where to?'

'To jail. Did you think we was goin' to have tea with the Mayor?'

I fumbled under the tables and finally found my hat. I could tell it — it was the one with the bullet hole in the crown. Practically a brand new hat, only three or four years old, and I had to come to New Orlando and get a hole shot in it.

The customers watched the Sheriff march me through the bat wings and onto the plankwalk. As we crossed the street to get to the jail, I said, 'This isn't a joke, is it?'

Jim Devers grinned. 'I told you there are certain people in New Orlando that you can't step on. Phillips is one of them. Besides, the bunks in the jail are better than the ones at the rooming house, and you wasn't goin' back to the Box-A anyway.'

★ ★ ★

It was a pretty good jail at that, as jails go. The Sheriff fixed me up with a couple of clean sheets and a blanket, and he even brought in a bottle of sour mash that he had been saving for a special occasion. He came into the cell with me and we sat up and talked for a while and nipped at his whiskey.

'It's what the folks expect,' Devers said wryly.

'You step on one of the Big Three and you've got to pay for it. You don't mind, do you?'

'I don't mind. I was ready to go to bed anyway.' The Sheriff grinned again. 'I've got a strong hunch that I shouldn't like you,' he said. 'You'll probably get me fired, or anyway ruin my reputation so that I'll never get re-elected.' He raised his glass. 'Well, I'm tired of the job anyway.'

We drank.

'If you need anything, just call my deputy. I'm going home and get some sleep.'

'I didn't know sheriffs had homes.'

'I've got a home, a wife and three

boys. A traveling cameraman came through about a year ago and got a picture of all of us. Frame and all, a dollar and ninety-eight cents. I'll show it to you sometime.'

He went out, leaving the key to the cell and his bottle of sour mash on the washstand beside the bunk. An honest sheriff with a wife and three kids. That was something to think about. It was better than anything else I had found in New Orlando.

★ ★ ★

I got up the next morning with a headache, a sore knee, and an ugly-looking bruise across the bridge of my nose. The morning was cold and sticky, and the sun hadn't made up its mind yet whether to come up or stay where it was. I used the key that the Sheriff had left behind and let myself out of the cell.

There was a deputy in the Sheriff's office, about to go to sleep with his boots on the desk. His eyes widened as I came

188

in. 'I thought you was in jail.'

'I was. Where's the Sheriff?'

'Home, I guess. Say, how did you get out?'

I tossed the key on the desk. 'You shouldn't leave these things around where the prisoners can get to them. If the Sheriff comes in pretty soon, tell him I'm up at the eating house.'

I left the deputy scratching his head, not quite sure if he ought to try to arrest me again or just forget about it. The streets of New Orlando were practically empty at this hour. A lonesome horse dozed at the hitching rack. A wagon was loading up with hay down at the livery barn. That was all.

I used the liveryman's pump to wash up before eating, then I came back through the barn to look at Dusty. The horse was happily munching corn out of a trough. He looked as if he had put on about ten pounds since I last saw him.

The wagon that had been loading hay pulled out and the liveryman came back to see who his company was.

'You didn't come back last night,' he complained, when he saw who I was.

'Couldn't, old-timer,' I said. 'I was in jail.'

His eyes narrowed down. He'd had me figured all along for a bad one. 'What you doin' out?'

'The Sheriff left me his key.'

He cackled. Maybe I wasn't so bad after all. 'Took good care of your horse,' he said. 'Be fifty cents more, though, for this mornin' feed.'

'That's all right,' I said. 'You figure out what I owe you and I'll come around and settle up after I eat.'

He wrestled a twist of tobacco out of his hip pocket and gnawed on it, looking slantwise at me from the corner of his eye. 'Heard they was some shootin' last night. Undertaker killed.'

'That's how the story goes,' I said. Then I thought of something. 'Say, were you awake when the shooting took place?'

'Reckon I was, why?'

'You didn't hear anybody leaving town

190

in a hurry about that time, did you? He had to leave this way. We thought we were chasing the killer north, but that turned out to be a blind alley.'

He thought about it, then shook his head sorrowfully. 'Can't say I heared a thing. I remember because the Sheriff asked the same question. Are you a friend of the Sheriff's?'

'If I'm not, I'd like to be.'

He nodded. We'd finally hit on some common ground — our respect for Jim Devers. I left the liveryman gnawing on that piece of tobacco, and went across the street to the eating house. I hadn't learned anything, except that maybe I had a liveryman on my side — if I ever needed a liveryman.

There was one more thing, though, but it wasn't exactly new. The man who killed the undertaker hadn't left town at all — anyway, not right after the shooting. He had made fools out of me and the Sheriff and then he had gone calmly about his business and mixed in with the crowd. That narrowed it down some but not much. Just about everybody I knew had decided to stay in town that night.

The eating house had just opened up and the cook and two waitresses were sitting on the business side of the counter drinking coffee as I came in. I took an end stool and called down to them. 'How about some fried mush, lots of butter and honey, and a side order of ham?'

The cook looked at me sadly and stopped blowing on his coffee.

'All right,' I said, 'I should have known better.'

'Steak and eggs comin' up.'

I was just getting my fork into the second egg when Sheriff Jim Devers came in. 'I trust you rested all right,' he said.

'Fine Have something to eat.'

'Just coffee. Had breakfast at home.' He called down to the waitress and she brought up a mug of coffee. 'Been talkin' to some of the posse members,' he said. 'They didn't find anything.' He rubbed his chin worriedly. 'Everybody's mad as hell about all these killin's. You don't happen to know where an ex-sheriff with a family could get a job, do you?'

He grinned as he said it, but his eyes said he was half-serious about it. I said, 'I don't think our killer left town at all. Anyway, not until things cooled off.'

He nodded soberly, not saying anything.

'How well acquainted are you with the badlands?' I asked.

'Pretty well. I've lived around here most of my life. If you're thinking of making a raid through that country, though, you'd better requisition a division of soldiers.'

'I know,' I said. 'I've seen part of the place. Just the same, some of the stolen cattle ought to be in there somewhere. The rustlers have to make several raids before they get enough together to make a drive. Now, if we could find out where they're holding the stock we could get some of the ranchers' cows back and probably pick up a rustler or two to boot. What we need is somebody to talk to.'

The Sheriff looked at me steadily. 'Just

how important is this job to you?'

'I'm about in the same fix you're in. If I want to keep working I have to bring back some of those cows and pick up some rustlers. Why?'

'Did you ever hear of a place called Sand City?'

I'd never heard of it, so he said, 'Well, it's almost a day's ride south and west of here, almost in the badlands. I've never been there, it's out of my jurisdiction. I tried it once but the Sand City Sheriff met me at the county line with a dozen or so deputies and wouldn't let me in.'

'You think if I went to Sand City I might find somebody to talk to? Somebody connected with the rustling?'

He shrugged. 'I don't know. It's just a chance, and we've tried about everything else. I'd better warn you, though, it's a long way down there, but it may be a lot longer coming back. You may not get back at all.'

'It sounds like a charming place.'

'It's not,' the Sheriff said flatly. 'Compared with Sand City, New Orlando is like one of those Paradise Islands that you see on picture calendars. If you don't come back, you won't be the first one. If you decide to go, that is. I can't go with you. It would have to be done on your own.'

We didn't say any more for a while. I finished my steak and mopped up the egg yolk with a biscuit. I left the usual silver dollar on the counter and the Sheriff and I went out.

'I think it would be better not to tell anybody where I've gone,' I said.

He looked at me. 'You're goin' to try it, then? All right, I won't say anything.' We stood there for a minute, watching New Orlando come up from under the covers. All towns at that hour of the morning are pretty much the same. We went across the street to the livery barn where I settled up with the liveryman and asked him to get Dusty rigged up.

'Leavin'?' he asked, as he brought the yellow horse out for me.

'Just for a day or so,' I said. He looked at me and then at the Sheriff, then he went into the barn and came out with a saddle boot and began to rig it up with my saddle. 'What's that for?' I asked.

He spat. 'You look like a man what might need a saddle gun. I ain't got nothin' but an old Smith breech-loader, but that's better'n nothin'.'

The Sheriff laughed. 'That's something I should have thought of. You wait here and I'll go down to the office and get my Winchester.'

When I climbed on top of Dusty I had my .45, a Winchester and four extra boxes of cartridges. I felt like a Mexican bandit after a raid on an ordnance warehouse.

'Don't wait to finish,' the Sheriff said, 'if things look bad down there. Come back and we'll think of something else.'

I told him I would take care of myself, and then I nudged Dusty and we moved out into New Orlando's Main Street and headed south. I looked back once and Jim Devers had that worried look on his face that didn't make me feel so good. Maybe I ought to wait awhile and think this thing over. But I didn't. The old liveryman was chewing thoughtfully and spitting and scratching the seat of his pants. I couldn't go back and face him after all the trouble he had gone to rigging up that saddle boot.

9

I took the road that went right through Ran Phillips' place. I didn't like the idea much — he'd probably thought up a trick or two by now to use on me the next time he saw me.

But I didn't see Phillips. I saw his house, though, a big white rambling affair, about the size of Northern's place but not as clean looking. From a distance the ranch house seemed to sag a little. It could have used a new coat of paint, too.

I went on past it, and across the creek, and onto the flat grazing lands to the south. There wasn't any road now, so I headed west until I could see those angry, naked hills of the badlands. The sun came up and I began to dry out. But it wasn't as bad as crossing the desert.

I passed through some of the small outfits — cocklebur ranches, they called them down here — and after a while there weren't any more ranches, or people, or cows, or anything else. I was too close to the badlands now for anything but prairie dogs, and maybe coyotes.

It was almost a full day's ride, as the Sheriff had said, if you wanted to get to Sand City. And the country was mostly baked clay with raw-looking gashes in it, and now and then a clump of bunch grass or a scrawny little blackjack. But if you keep going, after a while you'll see the town hunched up on the bald prairie.

There were only about a half a dozen buildings — sorry frame knock-ups leaning with the prairie wind — and no houses at all, as far as I could see. That's always a bad sign. Houses somehow represent family, and permanence, and a kind of respectability, and when you run onto a town without any houses, you know that those things aren't there. There were four buildings in one string, and sitting off a way, two more, and the piece of prairie in between, I guess, was Sand City's Main Street.

Six or eight horses dozed at a hitching rack in front of one of the buildings.

A saloon, probably. As I rode through the town I noticed that there was a post office, although the town probably didn't get mail more than twice a year; a harness shop, a feed store, an eating house and a couple of saloons. That was Sand City, a little town sitting on the edge of the badlands, dying in the hot Texas sun.

I pulled Dusty up and left him with the other horses at the hitching rack.

The saloon was about what you would expect in a town like that; dark and dank-smelling, in spite of the hot winds coming through the front door; as ugly and barren as the country it was built in. No mirror over the back bar, no pictures on the walls. Nothing but a scattering of tables and chairs, and the unhealthy smell of smoke and stale beer and unwashed bodies.

There were about a dozen rock-faced customers, some of them with guns on both hips. They didn't let me break up the party. They kept talking and laughing as I leaned on the bar and asked for beer, but I could feel them watching me, shooting quick little glances when they thought I wasn't looking. The beer came in a glass mug. It was soured. I held it up to the light and could see things swimming in it. I shoved it back and told the bartender I'd try the whiskey.

'What's the matter?' he said. 'Nobody never gagged on that beer before.'

'They have now. Let's have the whiskey.'

He didn't like me much. I didn't like him either. He was about two hundred pounds of ugly, sweaty blubber. Looking at him made me want to take a bath with lye soap.

But he brought the whiskey. He poured into a tumbler and shoved it to me. I sipped on it and listened to the mumbled conversations in the room. Loud enough to hear but not loud enough to catch what they were talking about. I poured again, and about that time one of the table customers got up and came over to where I was.

'You made Rosy kind of mad,' he said, grinning. 'He's been waiting close to six months for somebody to come in and buy that beer off of him.'

'I don't like beer much, anyway,' I said. 'I was thirsty after a stretch of riding.'

'You just come into town, didn't you?' he asked.

I grunted, not wanting to say anything wrong. He was a blonde-haired kid, about twenty-one years old, maybe twenty-two. He would have been good-looking if he hadn't let his hair get too long — it came almost to his shoulders — and if his cool blue eyes had had a little more life in them. He was one of the boys with a gun on each hip.

'You come from the north?' he asked pleasantly. 'Through New Orlando, maybe?'

Grunt.

'You're not very talkative, are you?'

I looked at him, waiting to hear what he might say next.

He laughed. 'I saw your horse out there. Good-looking buckskin. Good-looking saddle gun, too. You look like a man in the business to me.'

'What business would that be?' I asked carefully.

He took it good-naturedly and laughed again. 'You don't have to be so close-mouthed around here, stranger. Everybody's in the business that comes to Sand City, one way or another. Are you looking for a job?'

'That depends on the work.'

'Are you particular?'

I looked him over very carefully. 'Why? Are you hiring?'

He didn't laugh this time, but he grinned. 'You've got a jaw that flaps like a steel trap,' he said.

I figured it was time to loosen up a little. Maybe the kid was just the man I wanted to talk to. I said, 'I never saw a game where they paid off on talk. But I can listen — if you want to buy me a drink.'

He looked me over, still grinning. 'By God, I never saw anybody just like you.' Then he flipped a silver dollar on the bar and called, 'Bring that bottle back, Rosy.'

The bartender brought the bottle

reluctantly. He frowned at the kid like maybe he thought he was doing too much talking. But the kid waved him away after he got the bottle. 'Well,' he said, raising his glass, 'here's to Indian agents.'

I shrugged, tried to keep my eyebrows from going up, and drank with him. Behind the bar, I heard the bartender clearing his throat nervously. 'Bobby . . .' he started.

The kid stiffened. Those blue eyes of his seemed to frost over. He turned to the bartender and said very softly, 'What did you call me, Rosy?'

'Mr. Stuart, I mean,' the bartender said quickly. He was sweating. But there was something on his mind and he was going to get it out. 'I mean,' he said, 'well, too much talk. The boss ain't goin' to like it . . .'

About that time the kid reached over the bar, grabbed the front of the bartender's shirt and slapped him three times across the face, whack, whack, whack. It sounded like he was whipping a stick

204

across a picket fence.

That was all there was to it. The kid straightened up and brushed his hands and forgot all about it. The customers didn't seem to notice anything.

'Maybe we ought to take a table,' the kid said mildly, 'where somebody's not sticking his goddam nose in all the time.'

We left the bartender rubbing his flabby face and looking as if he was about to cry, and went over to a wall table. We sat there for a minute just giving each other a good going-over. I'd never seen him before. I'd never heard of him. But after a while I sat back and tried to get some awe in my voice as I said, 'Well — so you're Bobby Stuart.'

He grinned. 'You've heard of me, huh?'

'A name like yours gets around,' I lied.

He just sat there enjoying it. He was somebody. He hadn't been too sure of it until now, but when a stranger comes riding in from nowhere and says he's heard of Bobby Stuart — well, that just about settled it. Before long he would be thinking he was another Billy the Kid, or maybe even John Wesley Hardin.

'This job you mentioned,' I said. 'I could use some money, if there's some money to be picked up without too much trouble. Of course, you'd have to swing it for me. I don't know anybody in this part of Texas.'

'I can swing anything I take a notion to,' he said cockily. 'Have you got a name?'

'Sure. Smith.'

He chuckled quietly. 'By God, I don't know what it is about you that I like. Maybe it's because you know how to keep your mouth shut.'

'I can keep my eyes closed, too,' I said. 'And I don't hear very well. My memory's not worth a damn for faces or names — especially faces or names that don't want to be remembered.'

He nodded appreciatively. 'Have you got a home?'

'Not exactly. I've spent some time on the border, though.'

He looked thoughtful and pleased. After a minute he said, 'Well, well. So they've heard about me down on the border. What do they say about me?'

'They say you're a quick man with a gun. Maybe the quickest.'

He liked that. He sat back and smiled. 'I like you,' he said abruptly. 'I don't know why — there are damn few people that I do like in this God-forgotten country. Do you want that job?'

'If the pay's good,' I said, 'and if I don't have to kill any U. S. marshals.'

'You'll do,' he said thoughtfully. 'The pay's all right, and we don't get any government in this county. As a matter of fact, we don't get any law at all.'

'That sounds all right,' I said. 'Where do I sign the payroll?'

We had a drink. The kid sipped his as if it was fine old wine. 'We'll have to talk to Coffman,' he said. 'He does the hiring and firing here in Sand City. There won't be any trouble, though, if I give him the word.'

'Is Coffman the boss?' I asked.

Those cool blue eyes got to be careful eyes. 'That's one thing we don't ask

207

questions about,' he said. 'You just draw your pay and do your job. If you don't want it that way, then we'd better forget about it right now.'

I was moving a little too fast for him and had almost stepped on his toes. I backed up and said, 'Just so I get paid. I don't care where it comes from.'

That seemed to satisfy him. He raised a hand and called, 'Two more drinks over here, Rosy.'

'Yes, sir, Mr. Stuart,' the bartender said quickly, not forgetting his manners this time.

We had our drinks, the kid sipping his, as he had the first one. I looked the place over again, but there was nothing there that hadn't been there before. The customers were all very elaborately minding their own business. Probably they had learned that it paid to leave the kid alone. The bartender was still giving me the steely eye every once in a while. He didn't like me. He didn't like the kid, either, but he had a healthy respect for him.

The kid shoved his chair back and got up. 'Across the street,' he said. 'That's where Coffman is. You want to go over and talk to him now?'

'Whatever you say.'

We walked out with curious stares on our backs, but that was all. We went across the street and into a harness shop where an eagle-beaked old coot sat tooling some leather on a saddle tree.

'Coffman in?' the kid asked.

The old man grunted. We went on through the shop and the kid banged on a door in the back and pushed it open.

There was a man sitting at a roll-top desk, making some entries in a ledger. He looked up and frowned as we came in. 'Can't you see I'm busy?' he said.

'Not too busy for this,' the kid said. 'Coffman, this is Smith — he's looking for a job and he's not too particular what kind of a job.'

The man at the desk sat back and groaned. 'Another Smith. We've got four Smiths on the payroll already. That's the trouble with you birds — no imagination. That's the reason you'll never get anywhere or amount to a damn — no imagination.' He looked me over and picked at me with quick, birdlike little eyes. He was a lean, hollow-chested, pale-faced man in his late forties, and it was even money that lung fever would get him before he was fifty, if a bullet didn't get there first. He didn't miss a thing — the way I stood, my hands, my face, the way I dressed. He paid particular attention to the worn wooden butt of my .45. He liked that. No fancy silver mounted guns for him. Just a plain ordinary killing machine — that was the thing. 'All right, Bobby,' he said. 'What about him?'

'He wants some quick money, that's all.'

'I mean, do you know him?' Coffman said impatiently. 'We can't sign up every saddle tramp that happens to ride through Sand City.'

The kid's cool eyes looked at my face. For a minute he wasn't quite sure if I was worth lying for. But he had already bragged that he could swing anything he took a notion to, and I guess it was a little late to change his mind. He looked levelly at Coffman and said, 'Sure, I know him. You don't think I'd bring a stranger in here, do you?'

Coffman sat back and thought it over. I don't think he entirely believed the kid, but he was going on his own judgment now. 'All right, Smith, where do you come from?'

'Here and there. Along the border mostly.'

'Name some names down there,' Coffman said.

I fished around in my mind and drew out a hard case that I'd heard about down there. 'Sid Maxwell,' I said. 'We used to ride together some, but I haven't seen him in a long time.'

Coffman relaxed and smiled. 'Well, this will be easy enough to check on. Sid's working with us now.' That knocked the wind out of me. Of all the bad men in Southern Texas, I had to pick the one that worked with the rustlers! 'Well,' I said stupidly, 'what do you know?'

I couldn't tell what Coffman was thinking. He sat there looking at me and smiling, and I hoped he couldn't hear my stomach as it curled up and growled and tried to climb into my throat. He turned his head slightly and said, 'Bobby, you go over to the saloon and tell Sid to come over here.'

'I don't think he's there,' the kid said.

'Well, find out where he is and get him.'

The kid shrugged and went out of the room. I pulled up a chair and dropped into it before my knees gave away. What was I going to do when Sid Maxwell came in and called me a liar? Try to shoot it out with them and light out for New Orlando? That was a long, long way to go. Too long, I was afraid. Maybe I ought to make a break for it now. I could over-power Coffman easy enough and get as far as the street . . . But it was still a long way to New Orlando.

So I sat and sweated. I could feel the sweat form on the back of my neck. It raked down my back like the edge of a knife.

I said, 'Well, well. Sid Maxwell.'

Coffman laughed. 'He came in two weeks ago, about three whoops and a jump ahead of a posse. We got our Sheriff out, though, and met the posse at the county line and cut them off. Sid's been with us ever since.'

'You got yourself a good man,' I said. My voice seemed to come from far away, but Coffman didn't appear to notice. He got a cigar out of a box, rolled it around in his mouth without lighting it. He looked like he wanted to light it, but he was afraid to. That's the way lung fever is.

He didn't ask any more questions. There was no need to. We were just killing time until Sid Maxwell came in. Then boots again, coming through the harness shop.

I should never have sat down, I thought. You can't shoot worth a damn sitting down. Before I could do anything about it, Bobby Stuart was in the room again, and he was alone.

He glanced at me in a disgusted way,

as if to say, 'These damn fools that send you out on wild goose chases!' To Coffman he said, 'Sid's out with the herd where I thought he was. He won't be back in until tomorrow morning.'

My breath whistled between my teeth as I let it out. Or I imagined it did. Nobody seemed to hear it.

'Well,' Coffman said, 'I guess it doesn't make any difference. If he wasn't all right he wouldn't just sit here and wait for Sid.' To me he said, 'Do you know what kind of job this is?'

I shook my head. I wasn't sure if my voice was working yet.

'Have you got anything against herding a few cows and not looking too close at the brands?'

I just grinned, and that seemed to be the answer he wanted.

'All right,' he said to the kid. 'Take him out of here. I've got work to do.'

I felt like an old man as we went through the harness shop again and onto the dirt walk. Things like that don't do a man any good. It turns your hair gray, makes your hands shake, wears your heart out from beating too fast. I took a long, deep breath of air and let it out slowly. Now I knew how condemned men feel when they get a last minute reprieve and learn that the hanging's not going to take place after all. At least, not right now. Tomorrow, when Sid Maxwell came back to Sand City, it would be different. But that was tomorrow.

The kid was grinning, 'I told you there wouldn't be any trouble. All I had to do was say the word.'

I tried to grin back. 'I guess you're a man it pays to know. I'll try to do something for you sometime.' We strolled into the wide, dusty street, and the kid was still feeling pretty good because he thought he had a reputation that reached far beyond Sand City. There was a milk can in the street that he had been kicking along ahead of him; then — without any warning at all — he pulled out his right-hand Colt and shot it.

It was nice shooting, although the range was pretty close. The can jumped like a startled cottontail and went rattling up the street. The big, round explosion of his gun seemed to mushroom in the late afternoon. Loud, but mushy-sounding, the way with most sounds on the prairie. We began to get an audience. Faces appeared in windows and doorways, and the saloon customers came out onto the dirt walk to watch, after they found out that it was just target practice.

The kid nodded toward the can and said, 'Go ahead.'

He had been noticing my .45 for quite a while now, especially the worn wooden butt, and I guess he was curious to know just how good I was. There didn't seem to be anything else to do, so I took my gun out and burned a cartridge at the can.

It wasn't much of a job, if you've done as much shooting as most stock detectives. The can jumped again and wobbled crazily toward the hitching rack. The kid gave me a quick glance with no particular meaning in it. 'Again,' he said.

So I shot the can again, nicking it on

the edge nearest the hitching rack and sending it jumping into the middle of the street.

The kid's gun blazed before the can hit the ground, and the shot-up piece of tin went wobbling through the air like a wounded duck.

'Say' I said' 'that's all right.'

He grinned. 'You want to try it?'

'No, thanks. I've seen enough. Shooting like that is a little out of my reach.'

The sun was going down and the light wasn't very good, but I still think I could have put another bullet in that can if I'd taken a crack at it. But a look at the kid's face told me it wouldn't be the smart thing to do. He was happy and that's the way I wanted to keep him. The boys in front of the saloon had caught the spirit of the thing and were yelling for me to try it. I guess they had already taken me in as one of their happy little band. They had seen me go over to the harness shop and talk with Coffman, and then saw me come out with the kid and take part in a friendly shooting match. That was enough for them.

It was enough for me, too. 'No, thanks,' I said again. 'I know when I'm out of my class.'

And maybe it was the truth, after all. The kid could shoot; there was no doubt about that. At thirty paces he could hit a jumping milk can. It's entirely possible to live a lifetime and never see shooting like that. Of course, shooting a tin can and burning down another gun fighter are two different things. Under pressure maybe he would go to pieces — but I doubted it.

So we went back to the saloon and the kid insisted on buying me another drink, secure in the knowledge that he was still the best gunman in Sand City. Maybe the best in Texas, for all he knew.

★ ★ ★

It got to be dark pretty soon. The sun lay big and red on the western horizon, then suddenly it fell into the badlands and went out. The fat bartender began lighting lanterns. Some of the customers began to ease out of the place, get their horses at the rack and ride off somewhere. Probably to keep watch on the stolen cattle, wherever they were.

I hadn't asked any questions yet. Maybe tonight when the saloon trade picked up again I could get somebody loosened up over a bottle of whiskey. All I had to do was wait and I'd find out. It had to be tonight, though. By morning I had to be out of Sand City.

The kid said he had a little business to attend to, and he went out, and after a while I saw him riding through the street with some of his friends. Maybe I should have tried to fall in with them and found out where they were going. But I didn't. I asked Rosy, the bartender, where the livery barn was.

There wasn't any, it turned out, after a lot of wheedling. Getting an answer out of Rosy was about as painless as pulling an abscessed tooth, but after a while I did find out that there was a corral at the end of the street where I could turn my horse in and get him fed. I took Dusty down and treated him to some corn. I inspected his hoofs and rubbed him down, and he seemed to be in pretty good shape. Whether he was good enough to run all the way to New Orlando, I couldn't tell.

It was almost eight o'clock when I finished feeding myself and got back over to the saloon. The kid was there, sitting at a table.

'I'll buy you a drink,' I said.

'I thought you was broke.'

'Not quite,' I said. 'Now that I've got a job I don't have to be so close.'

He laughed. 'All right, if you want to throw your money away on Rosy's rat poison. 'He waved toward the bar and Rosy came over with a bottle.

I raised a glass and said, 'Well, here's to the Indian agents.'

That was starting a little fast. Maybe a little too fast. The kid's head jerked around after he cut me up and down with those cool eyes. 'What made you say that?' he asked carefully.

'No reason in particular,' I said. 'Because you said it this afternoon, I guess. Does it mean something?'

His mind went back to the afternoon, trying to remember if he had said anything about Indian agents. At last he did remember, and everything was all right again. He wasn't quite as happy as he had been before, though. 'Yes,' he said slowly, 'it means something. But it's one of those things we don't talk about.'

'We'll forget it, then,' I said. 'I didn't mean to bust in on somebody's secret.'

He grinned. That was more like it. 'Hell,' he said, 'it doesn't make any difference, I guess. You're hired on the job now, just like the rest of us, and you'd find out sooner or later. You know the cattlemen up around New Orlando sell their beef to the Indian agencies, don't you?' He chuckled quietly.

'When they've got some beef to sell, that is. Well, let's look at it this way — say you were in charge of buying beef for the Indians. The Government furnished you so much money to buy so much beef.

So you scrabble around for a few years, dealing with the cattlemen and trying to live on the wages the Government pays you — then one day you get an offer. Somebody wants to sell you the same beef you've been buying, at half the price. What would you do?'

'I'd probably get a bad case of eye trouble,' I said. 'So bad that I couldn't even see the brands on the bargain cows.'

He smiled and spread his hands on the table. 'That's the way it is. We go up north and collect our cattle, then we herd them until the Agent has another issue to fill. It's nice and easy. Do you think I'd get stuck in a place like this if it wasn't easy?'

I told him it sounded like my kind of deal. If it was good enough for a man with Bobby Stuart's reputation, it was good enough for me. That was the kind of talk he liked to hear. So I kept feeding it to him, along with the whiskey.

'Have you ever been in Abilene?' he asked suddenly.

I said I was up there about a year ago.

He poured another drink and stared into it moodily. 'That's one place I want to go,' he said abruptly. 'They're supposed to be goddamned tough up there. Hard cases like Ben Thompson, Hickok, Hardin — I hear they've got the run of the place.'

'They're pretty hard boys, all right,' I said.

He had another drink and began to get that glassy stare in his eyes. I had seen a thousand just like him — the more they drink the tougher they think they are. Boot-hills are full of boys like that.

'I'd like to see just how tough they are,' he said sullenly. 'Take Hickok; he's not bullet-proof, is he? Open a hole in him and he bleeds like anybody else. I don't see how they're so damn tough.' He poured again. 'You saw me shoot today. Do you think they shoot any better than I do?'

I thought about that for a minute, trying to picture in my mind what would happen if Bobby Stuart ever went up against men like that. Ben Thompson probably wouldn't even waste a bullet on him. If the kid got bothersome, Thompson would crack his skull with the butt of his .45 and forget about it. Hickok? The long-haired Marshal could kill the kid seven different ways and never set his glass down. And Wes Hardin, the deadliest gun fighter of them all — I didn't even want to think about a meeting like that.

'What the hell are you grinning about?' the kid demanded.

'I was just thinking,' I lied, 'that it would be quite a war. If you could wrangle one of those boys into a fuss, that is. I guess not even Hardin would be anxious to grab leather with Bobby Stuart.'

The kid's eyes widened. 'You mean they've heard about me up in Kansas?'

'Hear about you?' I laughed. 'You don't even know how famous you are.'

He could hardly believe it, and I couldn't blame him. It was going to take a lot of clean living to smooth over a lie like that.

'Well, I'll be damned,' he said finally.

'Clear up in Kansas, huh?'

I laughed again and poured him another drink. He couldn't get over it. He sat there staring at his drink, and at that minute he was probably imagining himself in the Bull's Head Saloon in Abilene, Kansas, calmly shooting the Marshal's revolver out of his hand, and scaring the daylights out of men like Wes Hardin, who could have carved forty notches in his gun butt, if he had been the kind of man to do such things. Bobby Stuart was seeing himself as quite a boy. But I was seeing him as just any other punk with too much ambition in the wrong places, who was born to be buried young in some shallow boot-hill grave with his boots on.

Looking at him was almost like opening the book to the future, and under Bobby Stuart's name seeing nothing but sudden death. I could almost feel sorry for him. But not quite.

About that time Rosy the bartender came over to our table and touched the kid on the shoulder. 'Mr. Stuart . . .'

He swallowed, and then went on determinedly. 'Don't you think you've had enough?' The kid reached up and knocked the bartender's greasy hand away. 'Get the hell out of here!' he said angrily. He half-stood up, glaring at Rosy. He was just aching to kill somebody — anybody. He suddenly had a reputation to live up to.

'Wait a minute,' I said very quietly and very easily. 'Rosy didn't mean anything. He was just kidding.'

The bartender's face looked like a poor grade of yellow candle tallow. He began backing up, swallowing fast, as if he had eaten something that was about to bounce on him. 'Yeah,' he said weakly. 'I was just kiddin', Mr. Stuart.' Then he turned and almost ran behind the bar.

The kid began to relax. He sat down slowly and reached for the bottle. 'Goddam bartenders,' he said, 'that can't keep their faces out of your business!'

The saloon, which had tightened up for a minute, started breathing again. Some of the peace-loving citizens thought up excuses and began drifting out of the place; the others went on about their business as if nothing had happened. The kid was getting a little too drunk to be comfortable around, but I couldn't tell if it was from the whiskey or from a misplaced sense of power.

'Well,' I said, trying to get the conversation headed back the way I wanted it, 'now that I've got a job, when do I go to work?'

'That depends on Coffman,' the kid said. His voice was a little fuzzy. 'Maybe tomorrow. Maybe the next day. Maybe not until we go north again to gather some more cattle.'

'About these cattle,' I said. 'Where do you keep them, anyway? Surely not in the badlands.'

I should have slid the question in sideways, I guess, when he wasn't looking. But whiskey and big ideas had him pretty well beaten down, and all he did was to give me a half-bored look with those eyes of his. 'Saddle Creek,' he said. 'That's the only place to hold cattle around here.'

I didn't know where Saddle Creek was, and I didn't want to push things too far by asking. Well, somebody in New Orlando would know where it was, so that didn't matter. But I still had the big question to go: Who was the boss?

Not Coffman, I knew that. Coffman was just somebody to receive orders and instructions from somebody else and pass them along to the hired hands like Bobby Stuart. Maybe the kid didn't even know who the boss was — probably he didn't. But Coffman would know. I thought maybe I ought to talk to Coffman again before I pulled out for New Orlando.

10

The kid hardly looked up when I left the table and went over to the bar to pay for the whiskey. He was deep in some boozy dream, swirling with gun smoke and death. Now that he fully appreciated himself, he couldn't be bothered with the likes of me.

But the bartender could. He was the suspicious one, the careful one. He had never taken me in, the way the others had done. I paid him, and he took the money and made the change, and those little buckshot eyes of his never left my face.

'Where's a place to bunk down for tonight?' I asked.

He turned his head and spat without taking his eyes off of me. 'Johnson House,' he said sourly, 'over the feed store.'

I said, 'Thanks,' and went out of the place before I leaned across the bar and hit him, the way the kid had done.

I walked down toward the feed store, just in case Rosy had his fat face against a window, but I didn't try to get a room in the Johnson House. I got Dusty out of the corral and hitched him loosely at the rack where he would be handy. Then I walked off in the darkness and came up behind the harness shop where Coffman had his office.

There was a lamp burning in the office, but the shop itself was dark. I went around to the back and could see Coffman still working on the books, all bent over across the desk. There wasn't any back door that I could see, just the little two-by-four window. That was going to complicate things some. I was going to have to go around to the front door if I was going to get in and talk to Coffman.

I eased around the side of the building and stuck my nose around the corner and had a look up and down the street. Nothing going on in the street. Over on the other side, the saloon was going full blast. I waited in the dark alleyway, trying to figure out another way to get in there. I wondered what my chances would be on hoisting my hundred and ninety pounds through that back window, while, at the same time, holding a gun on Coffman. Then some clouds passed under the moon and almost total darkness fell on Sand City.

That was my chance. I stepped up to the dirt walk and pounded on the door of the harness shop. Nothing happened. I pounded again, louder. I wasn't afraid of anybody in the saloon hearing anything, not in that uproar. 'Coffman, this is Smith, the man you hired today. Let me in.'

Nothing but silence on the inside.

What had happened in there? He must have heard me. I knocked again and got nothing again for an answer. Maybe he was asleep. Maybe, but I couldn't believe it, with the noise I was making. Maybe he had got suspicious and was waiting behind the door with a gun in his hand. Well, there was a way to find out.

I tried the door and it was latched

on the inside, so I went back into the alleyway and felt around until I found a good-sized rock, and about that time my covering clouds moved on toward Kansas, and the moon came out again. There in the moonlight I felt as naked as a skinned squirrel. But I went back to the door anyway and knocked the latch off with the rock. I stepped inside with my gun in my hand, expecting almost anything. What I found was just a dark empty harness shop.

'Coffman.'

No answer. I closed the front door and stood in the darkness for a minute, smelling the rich brown leather hanging somewhere in the shop. A little sheet of lamplight was laid out in the back of the place, coming from the crack under Coffman's door. Well, I thought, we can't carry this thing on all night. There were a couple of little clicks in the darkness as I thumbed the hammer back on my revolver. Then I felt my way to Coffman's door and opened it. He was still sitting at the desk, all bent over, the way

I had seen him through the window. He hadn't moved. He wasn't going to move.

His arms were folded on the big ledger, his head lay in his arms, and his wide-open eyes were staring at some point about six inches over my head. I went over and felt of the back of his neck, then jerked my hand away as if I had reached into a hole and got hold of a snake. He was cold and damp and sticky. He had been dead for at least three hours.

I must have stood there for a full minute, just staring at him. The open pages of the ledger were sprayed with a fine mist of blood, and there was blood on Coffman's lips and more on the floor. A long cigar ash under the desk told the story.

All the while time was passing. I became aware of it pretty soon. Well, I wasn't going to learn anything from Coffman. I wasn't going to learn any more from anybody, probably. The smart thing to do would be to get out of that room and out of Sand City as fast as I could find Dusty and get in the saddle.

But instead, I slipped the ledger from

under Coffman's dead weight and began going through it.

It didn't tell me anything. All the entries were made in code of some kind — a lot of scrambled letters and numbers that didn't mean anything to anybody but the man who put them there. And Coffman wasn't telling. I went through the book from front to back. A lot of entries. Probably a complete record of every cow that had been stolen, the brand it bore and the price it brought. But I couldn't be sure. I was wondering if I should try to get that book back to New Orlando and let somebody smarter than me work on it — and then I heard it.

It was just breathing. Inhale — exhale. Somebody breathing very quietly.

It wasn't me.

It sure wasn't Coffman.

I stood there for a long minute, telling myself not to do anything sudden. Just take it easy. Wait until my heart started pumping again, then turn very slowly and carefully and say hello to my company. I still had my gun in my hand. I didn't know what to do with it. I couldn't very well turn and try to outshoot somebody who probably had a gun aimed at my back. I could have, but it would just be buying a one-way ticket to a funeral. So I waited until somebody told me what to do.

'Just put your gun back in your holster,' Bobby Stuart said. 'Slow and easy. That's the way. Now turn around the same way.'

He didn't even have me drop the pistol on the floor. That was a nice touch. A touch that nobody but a wild-eyed kid would have used. But I did as he said.

'There,' he said, smiling. 'You're some boy, aren't you, Smith — or whatever your name really is? Now what did you have to go and kill Coffman for?'

I swallowed a couple of times. There he was, standing in the doorway, with two bone-handled .45's zeroed in on my belt buckle. He didn't look drunk at all — but his long blonde hair was wet and dripping and I guessed that he must have held his head under a pump to sober up.

I said, 'Hell, I didn't kill anybody. Go over and have a look for yourself. Coffman fired up a cigar and started coughing, and then he bled all over the place and died. I didn't see it, but that's the way lung fever works, especially the galloping kind that he had.'

The kid wasn't entirely convinced. 'Rosy,' he called without turning his head, 'come on in here!'

The fat bartender came padding through the harness shop and into the office. He looked at me and sneered. He went over to the desk, rolled Coffman around some and said, 'Hemorrhage, all right. No bullet holes in him.'

The kid was a little disappointed, but he kept on smiling. 'Well, it really doesn't make any difference,' he said to me. 'You're still in a bad way, mister. Rosy kept an eye on you after you left the saloon. You took your horse out of the corral and left him at the rack, which struck Rosy as kind of funny. Then he saw you come out of the alley, go up to the harness shop and knock the door in. He thought maybe I ought to look into it, so I came over and find you standing over a dead man and going through the books. Doesn't all that strike you as kind of funny?'

'I don't see anything funny about it,' I said. I tried to sound annoyed. Maybe I only sounded scared. 'I wanted to talk to Coffman about my pay, but when I knocked he didn't answer. When he didn't answer the second or third time I figured something must be wrong, so I knocked the door in to find out. I didn't kill him. You can see that.'

That was pretty watery, but I might have made it stick if the kid hadn't had the clincher to the thing. He holstered his left-hand gun, reached into his shirt pocket and took out a dirty white envelope. 'There was something I forgot to tell you.' He grinned. 'Rosy went to your horse, plundered around in your saddle pouch and found this.'

It was that letter. The one from John Barlow, the president of the Cattlemen's

Association, that had brought me to New Orlando in the first-place. I must have stuck it away in my saddle pouch and forgot about it.

There wasn't much to say after that. I just stood there wondering if it was too late to learn to pray, waiting for the roof to fall on me. Rosy was enjoying it. He backed over into one corner of the room to get out of the line of fire. He sneered at me again. He almost laughed.

'A stock detective,' Bobby Stuart said softly. 'Reagan, the letter says. Well, it doesn't make any difference, because no name's going to get carved on your tombstone anyway.'

Then he did the damnedest thing. He holstered his other gun.

I didn't get it for a second or two. He had me cold. All he had to do was pull the trigger. But instead, he holstered his guns, starting us both from scratch. I began to get it then. Maybe if Rosy hadn't been there it would have been different and he would have had me turn around and shot me in the back. But he had a witness now. And he had a reputation to live up to. He was probably remembering that shooting match we'd held earlier in the day — he'd outshot me that time, hadn't he? There was no reason why he couldn't do the same thing now. Anyway, I guess it appealed to his bloated ego to be able to give a man an even start before he cut him down.

Yes, sir, he'd be quite a hero after this was over. He'd go over to the saloon and calmly file another notch in his gun and tell how he'd given me all the chances in the world. And he would have Rosy to back him up. A stock detective! He didn't like stock detectives anyway. The more he thought about it the more he liked the idea.

Maybe a single tick of time passed by while all that went through my mind. And I stood there waiting for him to make his move.

There wasn't time to be nervous or scared. One, two, three, the seconds ticked by, and then it was all over. He made an innocent gesture with his left hand, lifting it slowly as if to brush his long hair away from his ear. I caught my eyes following that hand. I caught them just in time, because his right hand was diving for his gun.

He was pretty good, at that. You can go a long way and not see them any better. He had a nice arm and wrist action, and there wasn't anything in his eyes to give him away. But I must have been wound up for him. That was Bobby Stuart's unlucky day.

My .45 got into my hand somehow and exploded just as the kid's muzzle was coming over the top of his holster. He slammed back, whirled all the way around, then went down to one knee. Then the other knee. He dropped his gun and ran two or three feet across the floor on his knees, going nowhere. Then he went over on his face and lay still.

I turned my gun on the bartender and his face turned an ugly shade of green. He tried to say something, tried to beg me not to kill him, but his voice wouldn't work. I should have shot him.

I told myself to go ahead and kill him and the world would be a better place for not having him among the living. But I couldn't do it. I was a little out of practice in shooting unarmed men, even men like Rosy. So I stepped over and knocked him down with the barrel of my .45.

I didn't wait to see if he was out. I just got out of there. I ran outside and down the street to where Dusty was, and by the time the curious ones began gathering in front of the saloon we were fogging our way out of Sand City.

So we had a start on them, but not much of one. Pretty soon I could hear them thundering after us, and I guessed that Rosy hadn't got any more than a headache and was already spreading the news.

I don't know what time it was when Dusty and I took our leave of Sand City. Midnight, maybe. Once in a while that big round face of a moon would come out from behind a cloud and look down on us, as if it was just a little curious about those damn fool humans down there scrabbling around, trying to kill each other. Then it would get bored and go into hiding again. Moonlight and black prairie darkness. I couldn't tell which was worse. When it was light they would shoot at us, and when it was dark there was always a chance that Dusty would step in a prairie dog hole. It looked like it was going to be a long, long night.

And it was. Dusty was a good horse, a fast one and a strong one, but he didn't have all the bottom in the world. He wasn't meant to cover twenty miles at a run, or even a gallop. So we put on a good spurt at first and pulled away from them, and I hoped that maybe we could lose them in the darkness. But that curious moon kept coming out at the wrong times and I would have to let Dusty out again and use up some more coal. I wasn't so much afraid of their shooting — nobody can shoot worth a damn on top of a running horse, especially at night. I was afraid they would get smart after a while and make me break Dusty down, and when that happened the end would be close.

I got away with it for a while — for what seemed like a long time. I would keep Dusty just ahead of them; when they began to fall back I would ease him up and we would coast along for a while, almost a walk. And then they would come again. If they had kept that up, if they had given me a chance to pace Dusty, I could have made it. But finally they got smart.

I couldn't tell how many horses there were back there. There must have been a dozen or more, though, running pretty well in a bunch. Then some wise boy on a speedy horse — a cutting horse, probably — spurted out in front of the bunch and came after us. His horse didn't last long at that pace, and pretty soon he fell out of the picture altogether, but he had made me extend Dusty and that was what he was after.

They kept that kind of thing up for maybe an hour. We got a chance to rest some between spurts, but those forced sprints were taking it out of that yellow horse of mine. I don't know how he lasted as long as he did. He was lathered up, and blowing, and grunting, and I didn't have the heart to use spurs on him any more. He would run until his heart gave out, because that's the kind of horse he was. And all the time those solid horses behind us, that had been allowed to pace themselves, were moving up.

The eastern sky began to get gray and I could see a ridge ahead of us. I figured maybe we would make the ridge, but that would be the end of the line. I would have to make some kind of stand after that.

I heard the shooting then, but I figured it was just my pals in the rear letting me know that they were still with me. I didn't look up. I was concentrating on riding light and making that ridge. As we started up the little slope it finally dawned on me that the shooting was coming from the front as well as the rear.

I started grabbing my saddle gun, and then I saw the line of horses and riders top the ridge. The riders put rifles to their shoulders and let go with a volley, then another one, like a troop of cavalry facing out an Apache ambush. At first I thought they were shooting at me. My guts crawled up and tried to hide behind my stomach and my stomach tried to hide behind something else — but then I saw one of the riders move out a little ahead of the others. He yelled at me and motioned me on as the bullets went whis- tling over my head. I almost broke down and cried when I saw who it was. It was Jim Devers, the New Orlando Sheriff.

Somehow we made it to the top of the grade and Dusty wobbled to a stop on the other side. I got out of the saddle and cut the sweat and foam from Dusty's shoulders and chest with my hand. I rubbed his legs and tried to soothe him and calm him down. The shooting was still going on. I didn't give a damn. All I cared about right then was that horse.

After a while the Sheriff came down to where I was; the shooting was still going on, but it had worn itself down to an occasional spasmodic popping.

'I never thought I'd be so glad to see a sheriff,' I said. 'From now on I'm going to have more respect for you people. I might even build a monument or something.'

He didn't say anything to that. He swung down from the saddle and began rubbing Dusty's quivering forelegs.

'Don't think I'm complaining,' I said, 'but I'll have to say that you sliced it pretty thin. This ridge was the end of the line. If we'd gone any further I'd have had to put the saddle on myself.'

'It's the county line,' the Sheriff said, 'this ridge. It's Sand City's country beyond here.' He stood up and began cutting the lather off Dusty's Ranks. 'I hate to see a horse treated like this — I guess it couldn't be helped, though. All I could do was to gather up a few boys and wait here at the county line. I figured maybe you'd get in trouble. You're pretty good at that kind of thing. By the way, did you learn anything?'

'I think so. Do you know where Saddle

Creek is?'

He scratched his ear. 'In the badlands some where, I think. It's dry, though. Dry all the time, except once in a blue moon.'

'Well,' I said, 'it must have water in it now. That's where the cattle are.'

He looked at me as if he thought I was lying. Then I told him about Bobby Stuart, and Coffman, and all the rest of it, and he began to nod his head.

I said, 'Do you know any of those birds?'

'I heard about Stuart. He's got a name as a hot shot around these parts. He's supposed to be pretty good.'

'Not the best, maybe, but I don't want to run into anybody any better. What about Coffman?'

'Heard about him, too, but that's all. He didn't have no great reputation as a brain. Anyway, he's never been seen around New Orlando, so that about knocks him out of the boss rustler's job. Didn't you get any ideas? No hint or anything about who's behind it?'

'Nothing,' I said. 'I don't think anybody

knew but Coffman and he was dead by the time I got around to asking him about it.'

We listened for a minute. The shooting had stopped. We went up to the crest of the rise and saw the rustlers backing off across the flats, one of them shaking a fist at us.

Jim Devers chuckled quietly. 'That's Matt Colbright, the Sheriff down in Sand City.' Then he sobered. 'I guess we can be lookin' for war between counties if things don't come to a head pretty soon. Dick,' he called to one of his deputies, 'you keep about ten men here and see that that Sand City bunch don't get across the line. Hold them off till nightfall. If things aren't cleared up by then, I guess it won't make a damn.'

'Are you getting an idea?' I said.

A sad look of disgust was my only answer. 'Well, anyway,' he said, as the two of us headed back for New Orlando, 'we've got a line on some of the cattle. What we have to do now is get them out of there.'

'I still don't see how they got them there in the first place,' I said.

The Sheriff grunted, as if his disgust was too profound to be expressed in piddling, ordinary words. We stopped by Phillips' place on the way to town.

Phillips was out somewhere, but we left word for him to come to New Orlando as soon as he was located, and for the other ranchers to do the same. We jogged on for about a mile, taking it easy because of Dusty. I wasn't feeling too good myself. It seemed like I was nothing but a kid the last time I had any sleep.

And that was the way it came to me. Riding along in the hot sun, about to doze off in the saddle, and suddenly my head jerked up as if somebody had bitten me. 'Well, I'll be damned!'

Jim Devers frowned. 'What's wrong with you?'

'I don't know. But something sure the hell is. The next time I see a doctor I'm going to get my head examined.'

'You look like a man that's about to

get an idea,' the Sheriff said.

'I feel like a man who should have got an idea two days ago. Why, that lying little she-wolf!'

The Sheriff's frown deepened. 'Now, look here, let's don't overdo it and bust a girth. Now what's this idea you're about to give birth to? And who's a she-wolf?'

'It'll keep a few more minutes,' I said, 'until we get back to New Orlando. There's something there I want to check on. If it comes out the way I think it will, maybe we can grab a loose end to this mess and go to work.'

The Sheriff was a patient man. He humored me. He shook his head only once, sadly, keeping his own private thoughts politely to himself. We rode in silence the rest of the way to New Orlando.

The old liveryman was waiting for us at the livery barn, and after he got one look at Dusty he decided he didn't like me after all. He came over and put a hand on the horse's neck, rubbed his chest, feeling the heartbeat. Then he glared at me. 'Look here,' he said bitterly, 'that's no way to treat a horse.'

I said, 'I'm sorry, old-timer, it couldn't be helped. How about taking him in and pampering him for a while? Have you got another horse I can use if I need one?'

He almost said no, but the Sheriff nodded to him and he grudgingly admitted that maybe he could rustle up one. Not much, though. A man treated horses like that, he didn't need much.

We left him talking to himself and went up the street toward the Star Bar. Past the Star Bar and on to the corner. Finally Jim Devers stood it as long as he could and was about to start asking a question. 'Just a minute,' I said. 'Wait until I'm sure about something.'

We went around to the Ferguson Funeral Parlor — except that it didn't belong to Ferguson any more. He died and left it to a man named Palmer, and Palmer got shot in the head because of his loose interpretation of the Law of Decency, especially when it came to pilfering his dead customers. Well, Palmer had paid for his sins. Wonder who was doing the undertaking these days, anyway?

We went up to the front door and knocked, but nobody answered. We tried the door and it was locked.

'Palmer's widowed sister came and took most of the furniture,' Jim Devers said. 'I guess she locked the place up, too.'

''Let's try the back door,' I said.

So we went around to the back, and that door was locked too. But I was too close now to let a locked door stop me. I backed off a little and raised my foot, smashing the heel of my boot against the latch and the door flew inward.

'Now wait a minute, Reagan!' the Sheriff said sharply. 'You can't go around kicking people's doors in.'

'You can if you're the law,' I said, 'and if you've got a good reason. You're the law. Come on in and maybe I'll show you the reason.'

He didn't like it but he followed me in. It hadn't changed much — the same old sawhorses and the same plank slabs where Palmer laid his customers out before boxing them up. The same zinc tubs stacked in the corner, and the coal oil lamp on the high mantel on the inside wall. That lamp was what interested me. I looked at it and grinned.

'Well,' the Sheriff said grimly, 'do you think you could tell me just why I'm violating private property?'

'Let's go back a way,' I said. 'Back to the night Palmer was shot to death in this room. You remember I came back here before you did to see if I could find something that would tag the killer. I didn't find that, but I did find Jane Albert here in the room with the dead man. She told me a story that I didn't take much stock in at first — said she had come in looking for her pa just as the shot was fired. After we left the place she was too scared to go into the back room right away, so she waited awhile and then tried it. When she finally got around to it the killer had blown out the lamp and was bending over Palmer and going through his pockets. Then the killer got away in the darkness and she couldn't see who he was.

'Well, she was scared stiff when I found her. There was no doubt about that. The lamp was burning again, though, and I asked her about that and she produced a match that she had frozen onto. A used match. Well, that seemed to settle it. I guess I didn't tell you about that, though. It must have slipped my mind.'

The Sheriff's face began to stiffen. Anger was finally going to work on him. 'It slipped your mind!' he said coldly. 'Maybe I'll throw you into jail and let it slip my mind where I put the key.'

'I'm sorry that I didn't tell you,' I said, 'but it didn't seem like anything then. Just a while back something started to bother me, and finally it hit me what it was. Look at that lamp.

'It's too high for her,' I said. 'She couldn't have lighted the lamp, so the lamp was never blown out. She went to a lot of trouble to make up a lie about that. She even got a match and struck it and held onto it to try to prove something or other. Anyway, she lied. There's no furniture in here that she could climb on to light the lamp, except those slabs, and the slabs were on the other side of the room; besides, they had dead men on them. You saw the stuff in the front room. It would take a blacksmith and two of his sons to move that kind of furniture.'

'All right,' the Sheriff said dryly, 'she lied about the lamp. Now do we know who the killer is?'

'Not yet, but we may before long. She must have had a reason to lie about the lamp. She either saw the killer and knew who he was and didn't want to tell us, or she went through Palmer's pockets herself and found whatever it is everybody's looking for. Whatever it is, it must point the killer out — except maybe he wasn't a killer before Palmer; just a rustler. Anyway, she didn't want to tell us who he was.'

'Why?'

'Because she's in love with him.'

The Sheriff looked at me, he looked

at the lamp, he walked around in a little circle, then looked at me some more. '*Who* the hell is she in love with?'

'I don't know,' I said. 'I didn't think she knew either, but I guess she did. Anyway, we've got it narrowed down to three now. Northern, or Phillips — or her father.'

Jim Devers groaned. 'Just between us, it's been narrowed down to three all the time, hasn't it?'

I shrugged. 'I guess so. But we didn't know which one. And we didn't know how to find out.'

'And we still don't know which one . . . ' And then he stopped. We didn't know, but Jane Albert did, and that had proved to be an unhealthy position for other people. I almost found out once and it had almost got me killed. Palmer did find out and it did get him killed.

The Sheriff said, 'Are you thinking what I'm thinking?'

'That maybe Jane Albert is next on the list?'

I couldn't very well believe that, but it

was an unnerving thought just the same. I couldn't believe that Northern would do it, or Phillips either; and surely George Albert could be counted out. Still, there were a lot of things we didn't know. I said, 'There's no use taking any chances. Let's take a ride out to the Box-A.'

We went out of the funeral parlor and around to Main Street. There was quite a collection of ranchers in front of the Sheriff's office — I had almost forgotten that getting their cattle back was going to make this quite a day for them. George Albert was there, and he motioned to us as we crossed the street. I didn't see Northern or Phillips anywhere.

'Is it true what they say?' George Albert asked, 'that you've located our cattle for us?'

'I think so,' I said. 'Some of them, anyway. Do you know where Saddle Creek is?'

'Why, yes,' he said. 'I was there once, but that was a long time ago. It was as dry as bone meal.'

'Well, that's where your cattle are supposed to be,' I said, 'so there must be water in it now. I'd suggest that the ranchers get their riders together and go down there as fast as they can. There may be some shooting of course, but now that you can concentrate your forces I doubt that they can give you much trouble. By the way, where's Northern and Phillips?'

He frowned just a little. 'I don't know where Northern is; I thought he would be here by now. Phillips came over to our place early this morning and wanted to talk to Jane. Jane wasn't there, though. She took that chestnut mare out almost before daybreak and hadn't come back.' His frown deepened and became worried. 'I don't know about that girl,' he said slowly. 'She — well, she hasn't been herself lately. I guess I don't understand young people very well. Even Marcia confuses me at times.'

'About Phillips,' I said, 'what happened to him?'

'Why, he rode out to look for Jane. When I heard that our cattle had been spotted I sent Vic out to look for both of them. I came on to town.'

I looked at Jim Devers and his jaw looked like it was set in concrete. 'Mr. Albert,' he said, 'I'll leave my deputies here and they'll go with you ranchers down to Saddle Creek. Reagan, I guess we'd better take that ride you mentioned.'

11

We didn't waste any time getting out to the Box-A this time. The liveryman had fixed me up with a spotted horse, a little sway-backed and not much to look at, but when it came to covering ground he was all right.

We tried the ranch house first, just on the chance that Jane Albert had come back. Marcia Albert seemed a little surprised at seeing me and the Sheriff together. I guess she had never thought of me as one to pal around with the law.

'Why, no,' she said, 'Jane isn't here now. She went riding early this morning. But I'm sure she'll be back before long, if you'd like to wait.'

That to the Sheriff. She hardly looked at me.

'Thank you just the same, ma'am,' Jim Devers said. 'We'll just ride around and see if we can find her. Do you know where she might be?'

Something was wrong — Marcia could tell that, but she didn't know what it was. 'Jane usually goes by the springs,' she said, frowning slightly. 'Sheriff, is anything the matter?'

'Not a thing, ma'am,' the Sheriff said heartily.

'We just wanted to talk to her. Well, we'd better go, Reagan.'

So we smiled and put our hats back on, and started off the porch. Then Marcia said, 'Mr. Reagan — if you have just a minute.'

I stopped and turned around. I thought I saw one of the Sheriff's eyebrows go up — he was interested, but not too interested to mind his manners. He went on back to his horse.

I said, 'Yes, Mrs. Albert.'

She blushed just a little. That was something she had learned since the old Bull's Head Saloon days. 'I'm not sure that this is the time or place,' she said, 'but something has been bothering me. I — well, I owe you an apology about . . .' Her voice trailed off.

'About the other night?' I said. 'Forget it. I have.'

'It's not easy to forget,' she said. 'I was so sure that you would tell him. You see, Mr. Reagan, I love my husband very much.'

And I guess she did. The past is in the eternal past, as they say, and all that counted was the future. Unless, maybe, you're a stock detective, without a future. I said again, 'Let's just forget it.' There didn't seem to be anything else to say. I was about to turn and walk off the porch, and out of Marcia Albert's life, I hoped, when I thought of something.

I said, 'Come to think of it, there's something that's been bothering me, too. I've run into a lot of loose ends here in New Orlando, things that seem to happen for no reason at all. My first night here two hard cases that I'd never seen before in my life tried to kill me. They don't tie in with the rustling in any way that we know about, so I've been wondering why they wanted to kill me.'

I waited, but she didn't say anything.

So I said, 'That happened not long after I met you in New Orlando. It occurs to me that maybe you were a little quicker than I was and recognized me right away. You were afraid I would tell your husband something when I finally got around to remembering where I'd seen you, so you hired the two hard cases to make sure that I didn't. Just to satisfy my curiosity, is that the way it happened?'

She looked at me steadily with those dark, cool eyes. She didn't say a thing. And that was the answer.

'Well, it doesn't make any difference now,' I said. 'I was just curious.' I put my hat on again and walked out to where the Sheriff was waiting.

'I didn't know you were chummy with Albert's wife,' Jim Devers said dryly.

I said, 'You can't exactly call it chummy — we just understand each other. Now let's get started north, toward those springs.'

★ ★ ★

It was another hot day. The sun blazed down and heat figures danced over the prairie, and the horses seemed to be running on treadmills and getting nowhere. But we finally raised the springs, and when we did we could see a lone rider close to the water.

'Can you make it out?' the Sheriff asked.

'It's not the girl,' I said. 'It's Vic Schuyler, I think, the Box-A foreman.'

When we got closer we could see that it was the foreman all right, red-faced and sweating rye whiskey from every pore. 'If it get's any hotter,' he said, 'damn if I don't go back to Dakota. What're you boys doin' out in the heat of the day?'

'Looking for the Albert girl,' the Sheriff said.

'Have you seen her?'

'Hell, no. That's what I'm doin' out here, lookin' for her. I didn't think it was important enough to get help from the Sheriff's office, though.'

'I just wanted to ask some questions,' Jim Devers said. 'You haven't seen Northern or Phillips, have you?'

'Not Northern. I saw Phillips, though, down south. He's lookin' for her too. Say, what the hell's goin' on, anyway, that a piece of a girl gets so important all of a sudden?'

The Sheriff and I looked at each other, thinking the same thing. If trouble came, Vic Schuyler would be a good man to have around.

Jim Devers said, 'To tell the truth, Vic, we're looking for trouble. We're not sure what kind, or where it'll come from, but it's ready to pop. We know that.'

The foreman frowned. 'You mean Northern and Phillips are gettin' ready to fight over that girl?'

'We kind of had the idea that one of them was getting ready to kill her,' I said.

Vic Schuyler stared at us. Suddenly he laughed. 'Now that's a hell of a thing! She's been askin' for it, though. She's done nothing but cause trouble around here as long as I've been on the Box-A. Which one of them do you think it is?'

'We don't know,' the Sheriff said. 'But you might be able to help us. Why don't you go down south and find Phillips and bring him here to the springs and hold him? Reagan and I'll scramble around to the east and see if we can pick up Northern and the girl.'

The foreman shrugged. 'Well, all right.' He pulled the battered carbine out of his saddle boot and squinted down the barrel. 'Been usin' it on wolves,' he said, 'but I guess it'll work on humans too, if things come to that.'

He pulled his horse around, squinting up at the sun, as if he hated the thought of riding into that heat again. But he rode. He booted the carbine, nudged his horse away from the water and headed south at a lope. As he topped a small rise I thought I could hear him laughing again. It must be comforting to have a sense of humor like that.

'We'd better split up here,' I said. 'If Vic Schuyler's already covered the south, that just leaves the north and east. She couldn't have wandered off too far.'

But far enough, the Sheriff was thinking. 'All right,' he said, 'we'll meet here at the springs when we find something.'

So the Sheriff headed east and I went north. There wasn't much above the water hole but the frayed-out end of the grazing land and the beginning of the desert, and why a girl would want to go for a pleasure ride in that kind of country I didn't know. But I scoured the ground pretty well, anyway, knowing that a girl like Jane Albert was capable of doing practically anything for no reason at all.

But she wasn't there. I kept riding until there was nothing to look at but sage and gravel and I decided that was far enough. The sun was beating down like it was out to set a record, and the whole thing began to seem pretty ridiculous before long. What kind of man would deliberately set out to kill a girl? The girl he was in love with, at that. Of course with hard cases like my pals Huck and Kramer, it was different — but with respectable ranchers, that was something else again. I began to feel a little silly about the whole thing. It was something a person might think up in a moment of panic, but after he's had time to let it settle . . .

That was when I saw the rider.

He was a long way off and I couldn't tell much about the man, but I thought I recognized the horse. It was a big black horse. I had seen Kyle Northern riding a horse like that. I couldn't think of anything else to do, so I stood up in the stirrups and waved. The rider waved back. And about a half a minute later a shout came drifting across the prairie, but by that time he was already headed in my direction.

When he got closer I saw that sure enough, it was Northern. And he wasn't riding at a slow, easy lope, the way you ordinarily ride when you just want to come over and say hello to a friend. He had the iron dug into that black horse and was streaking across the prairie like a cayuse with high-life under his tail.

I wasn't sure what to do — whether to meet him with a gun in my hand, or just take it easy until I found out what was going on. While I was thinking about it he pulled up in a cloud of dust. I said,

'It looks like everybody all of a sudden lost interest in their stolen cows. Are you looking for the Albert girl, too?'

'I am,' he said. 'Have you seen her?'

There was a grim set to his jaw and an uneasiness in his eyes that I decided I didn't like. I thought that maybe this was the time to get my gun out. But I didn't. And then that black horse skittered around and I saw something I hadn't seen before.

It was in the saddle boot and I couldn't see much of it except the stock and the rear sight. It looked like it might be a Winchester. I wasn't sure about that, though. But I was sure about that rear sight. It was a Buffington's windgage, a leaf sight that army sharpshooters use when they want to knock somebody down at twelve or fourteen hundred yards. On a good rifle it could be a deadly little gadget, but I hadn't seen one in a long time. It was a little too fancy for the ordinary cowman, and besides, somebody might accuse him of bushwhacking inclinations if he was caught with a rig

269

like that.

It was kind of a shock seeing somebody riding around with such an outfit in
his saddle boot, the situation in Orlando
County being what it was. I didn't do
anything for a few seconds. That damned
windgage fascinated me. I just sat and
stared at it.

In the back of my mind I knew that
I was looking at a gun that had almost
brought Pat Reagan to a bloody end,
and I must have realized that Northern
had been the man behind the gun.

I stared. I should have been grabbing
for my .45.

By the time I got around to it, though,
it was too late. Northern had thought of
it first. I looked up and I was staring into
the muzzle of Northern's own revolver,
and he was shaking his head sadly from
side to side, like a man who has just discovered a nasty job that's got to be done,
and he doesn't like it at all. But he's going
ahead and do it just the same.

We stared at each other for a minute
and I said, 'Well, well.' That was all I

could think of. My stomach was beginning to crawl around again, and the sweat on my back felt cold. So this is the way you face death, I thought, with a sick stomach and a cold back. Well, I guessed, it could be worse. I hadn't broken down and started bawling yet.

It never occurred to me right then that I wasn't going to die. It was either me or Northern, and Northern was the one with the gun in his hand, so it wasn't going to be him.

So with the end as a dead certainty, I sort of lost interest in it. I began to think about all the things I had done wrong and wonder if they could have been done any differently. I had gone off onto some bad trails, all right; for one thing, I had wasted too much time chasing my tail with Huck and Kramer, when they hadn't had anything to do with rustling. Then there had been Jane Albert to complicate things — who was still complicating things, for that matter, but I probably wouldn't have to worry about that. I looked toward the rise, half-heartedly hoping to see Jim Devers or Vic Schuyler come charging in to the rescue, like the last chapter in a dime novel. All I saw was a ripple of dancing heat waves.

Then Northern said, 'I'm sorry it had to end like this, Reagan. I haven't got anything against you, except that you came around meddling in things that were none of your business.'

He spoke quickly, but softly, like a man in a hurry to get out of the house but not wanting to wake the baby.

I said, 'Rustling is my business. I get paid to stop it.'

He looked at me sadly, as if he thought I had made a big mistake by not taking up bricklaying as a profession. He said, very slowly, as if it was very important to impress me with the seriousness of the matter, 'I want to know where Jane is. I want to know now. I'll trade you your life for that information; that's how important it is to me.'

I believed him. That's how deadly serious he was. If I could have told him where the Albert girl was, he would have let me go — for a little while, anyway. Until he could get my back in that Buffington's sight again. But I had to say, 'I don't know where she is, and if I did know I wouldn't tell you.'

His .45 wavered just a little, like maybe he was thinking about letting me have the barrel across the face. Then it steadied. 'All right,' he said, 'where's Vic?'

'Vic Schuyler? Why?'

Anger and impatience seemed to drain all the blood from his face, but somehow he managed to hang onto himself. 'Goddam it, Reagan, can't you see I'm serious about this? I want to know where Vic Schuyler is.'

'And I want to know some things myself,' I said, and anger was beginning to get a hold of me, too. 'That rifle in your saddle boot — that's the one you tried to shoot me in the back with, isn't it? All right, that ties things up into a neat little package, but there are still a few loose ends that I haven't been able to grab. You tried to kill me because you were afraid I was going to find something in Kurt Basser's boot. But you missed, and I didn't find it — but the undertaker found it and you killed him. It all ties together, but the whole thing hinges on the bushwhacking, and I can't prove that. Not even with that fancy killing equipment you've got there. Now, just to satisfy a condemned man's curiosity, do you want to admit what I've guessed at?'

'Go to hell,' he said hoarsely. 'Where's Vic Schuyler?'

His gun hand was beginning to whiten around the knuckles, which is a bad sign, but I figured he would hold off a while longer, as long as he was still asking questions. 'So you killed Palmer,' I went on, 'but it wasn't as nice and clean as you would have liked it. Jane Albert saw you. The next logical step would be to get rid of her before she loses her nerve and turns loose with everything she knows. Were you planning to use that rifle, Kyle? It would be neater that way, wouldn't it, at a distance?'

I shook him with that one. He stared at

me with those clear blue eyes, his mouth slightly open in surprise. 'Do you really believe that?' he asked tightly. 'Do you think I would hurt her, for any reason in this world?'

Until then, I had thought it. I was almost sure of it. Now I wasn't so sure. 'All right,' I said. 'What kind of an answer do you get?'

'It's Vic Schuyler. He's the one out to kill her. Can't you get that through your head?'

I must have looked funny then. I felt funny. Kyle Northern, with all the evidence in the world piling on him, and there he sat accusing Vic Schuyler, whose only crimes, as far as I knew, consisted of being a little crazy about his boss's wife and drinking too much rye whiskey. I said, 'You're going to have to think of a better one than that when the boys start shaking out their hanging ropes. I've seen a lot of rustlers and they all boil down to the same type — greedy, mostly, wanting something bad and not caring how they get it. That could fit you.

You want money and position here in Orlando County, and before things got too far along maybe you wanted to marry Jane Albert. But not Vic. He's got plenty of rye whiskey and that's everything he wants — almost. The foreman's too easygoing. He's not the type to be a rustler, so that lets him out of the killings, too, and you'd better think of somebody else to . . .'

It was quite a speech and I was just getting warmed up when Kyle Northern leaned a little out of the saddle and crashed his Colt's .45 on the corner of my jaw.

I hardly felt it. Suddenly the sun went out, and that was all there was to it.

* * *

I came out of it slowly. I had been through this once before and I knew just what to do. I didn't do anything. I lay quiet and concentrated on breathing for a long while. Finally I opened my eyes. The sudden light blinded me. I closed them

276

again, and after a while I turned over so I wouldn't be looking at the sun. I got my elbows under me, I got my knees under me, and then I crawled around in a small circle, spitting blood. I didn't feel any bullet holes in me anywhere. I couldn't see any blood except what came from my split cheek. I couldn't understand why he hadn't killed me. Or maybe he had, and here I was crawling around on the floor of Hell.

It was too hot for that, though. It couldn't be anywhere but West Texas on a gentle summer day. Well, I'd had about enough. If I could just find my horse I'd ride the hell out of here and leave New Orlando to the boys with harder heads than mine. Northern could go on with his rustling, and Albert could keep writing letters to the Cattlemen's Association, and Jane Albert could go on playing both ends against the middle. The hell with it.

All of which was fine, but something kept bothering me. Oh, yes, Vic Schuyler. How did he get into a thing like this, anyway? Why did Northern accuse a hard-working, easygoing guy like that? Why not Phillips? Or even Albert? Vic Schuyler didn't make sense.

The foreman must know something, though. Else Northern wouldn't be so eager to line him up in that windgage sight of his. Then a thought hit me and chilled me — what if Northern had already done away with Jane Albert, and now he was out to kill the foreman and lay everything onto the dead man? That was something to think about. But why hadn't he killed me too? I didn't know, but there was a way to find out. I hated the thought of a man like Vic Schuyler going down under a sniper's rifle — and anyway I owed the foreman something for all that whiskey of his that I'd used. The least I could do was to find him and warn him.

I started thinking about getting up.

It was a long job, and a hard one, but finally I made it. I got to my feet and practiced walking. That spotted horse that the liveryman had rented to me was about a hundred yards across the prairie, nibbling at a scrawny little blackjack. I tried calling to him, but it didn't work. I had to walk it.

Finally I corraled that spotted horse, climbed on board and we headed south again at a nice, easy walk. The sun could fall, countries could perish, cities could vanish, but nothing was going to get that horse out of an easy walk. Not with my head in the condition it was in.

It took some time but finally we made it back to the springs. Nobody was there. Just the cottonwoods and the cows. I watered my horse and had a drink myself and washed my face. I felt a little better. I walked up to some higher ground and saw a rider heading toward us under full steam.

It was the Sheriff. 'Hell's broke loose,' he shouted, as soon as he got within hollering distance. 'Did you find anything?'

'I found Northern,' I said. 'He left me this little souvenir on the side of the face and rode off somewhere. He didn't say where.'

Jim Devers swore. 'It looks like Northern, all right. I found Phillips; he's up a way in a gully with a bullet hole in his leg. He says Northern did it.' I began climbing in the saddle again and the Sheriff went on. 'According to Phillips, he came out this morning, like Albert said, to see the girl. Here's something I didn't know about — he says he's going to marry Jane Albert.'

That shook me. 'Phillips? She's a crazy one, but I had the idea she would turn to Northern, if anybody.'

The Sheriff shrugged. 'That's what Phillips says. They agreed last night, according to him. Phillips claims the Albert girl was afraid of Northern — had been for a couple of days. If it's true, that puts your funeral parlor story in a better light.'

'Did Phillips say anything about Vic Schuyler?' Jim Devers frowned. 'What about Vic?'

'I think we'd better find him,' I said. 'I don't know why, but I think Northern's out to kill him too. By the way, Northern's carrying a fancy rifle with a sharpshooter's sight on it. How did Phillips get shot?'

'He says he found the Albert girl this morning and was coming back to the house when they ran into Schuyler and Northern having a big argument. Phillips sent the girl back and butted into the argument himself. He doesn't know what it was about. The girl was out of sight by that time, and when Northern started after her, Phillips tried to stop him. That's how he got shot.'

I said, 'There's something crazy as hell. Vic didn't say anything about all this when we saw him a while back.'

The Sheriff said, 'I think that's one reason we'd better start looking for him.'

12

We found Phillips in a little draw about a mile north of the springs. He was taking on in a bad way, but nothing to call the undertaker about. A .45 bullet had messed up the upper part of his right leg and he had lost quite a bit of blood, but the bone didn't seem to be broken. The Sheriff had a canteen on his saddle, so we left that with him and rebandaged the wound with a piece of his shirt tail. He lay there cursing bitterly and earnestly. He seemed a little out of his head.

'You haven't got any idea where Northern could be, have you?' the Sheriff asked. 'Or the girl?'

He just stared at us with glassy, angry eyes.

The Sheriff shrugged. 'I guess we'll have to leave him for a while.'

So we rode on south, bearing west a little toward Hound Dog Creek. It was strictly hit or miss now. It was a little late to go back above the springs and pick up Northern's trail and follow him. I should have thought of that earlier. But I hadn't. Where was that girl, anyway? The ground had been pretty well covered and somebody had to stumble across her before long. If somebody already hadn't, that is.

Finally we came within sight of the creek, but there still wasn't anything to be seen of any of them. Up ahead there was some high ground that looked like it might be a good place to size things up from. We headed for it.

From the high ground we got a pretty good view of the southern part of Orlando County, but that was about all. We could see the green horsehoe bend of Hound Dog Creek as it twisted behind Phillips' place and ambled off toward the badlands. We could see another hill about a half-mile off — a curious sort of bald formation with three or four big rocks sitting right on top of it. All around it was the wide, green stretch of grazing country, dotted here and there with bunches of cows.

Pretty enough country, bright and shimmering in the heat of that West Texas sun — but suddenly I wasn't interested in the scenery. About that time Jane Albert broke out of the creek brush and came riding toward us.

She had that little chestnut mare of hers let out all the way, and they were burning a dusty swath across the prairie. They didn't seem to be traveling so fast, though, because they were a long way off. With that dust streamer playing behind them, they looked like something caught up in a lazy desert whirlwind, just playing around and not getting anywhere in particular.

'By God,' the Sheriff said, 'that's the girl, Reagan!'

We put some iron to our horses and began going down the slope to meet her. That was when we saw the other rider come fogging it out of the lowland around the creek and head toward her. It was that big black horse again. Kyle Northern.

The Sheriff put one hand to his

mouth and bellowed for Jane Albert to turn back. Then he yelled at Northern to stop. But Northern wasn't stopping that day. He cut across our path like a one-man stampede, and the Sheriff burned a couple of cartridges in his direction, not doing any good.

'Let's get him, Reagan!' Jim Devers called. 'Our luck's strung out too far to have it snap now!'

We tried, but that spotted horse of mine was no match for Northern's black. Neither was the Sheriff's horse, for that matter. The rancher cut in front of us, about a hundred yards off, and began burning up the ground in the direction of that bald hill we had been looking at. That struck me as funny. Jane Albert had got turned around by now and was headed back toward the sheltering brush of the creek, but Northern wasn't going after her. He was headed straight for the hill.

Somewhere in the confusion of things, I heard a rifle bark, flat-sounding in the bright afternoon. It wasn't the Sheriff —

he didn't have his rifle with him, and neither did I. It wasn't Northern, because he was riding hell-for-leather, not seeming to give a damn for anything except getting to that hill. It looked like somebody else had come to the party.

The rifle sounded again, and this time I saw it. Not the rifle, but the bullet — or where the bullet hit, anyway. I was looking at Jane Albert when it happened. The rifle cracked and that little chestnut of hers crumpled in full stride, going head over heels. Girl and horse got mixed up and lost in a cloud of dust, and I didn't try to separate them. If she was lucky she would be thrown clear and get away with no more than a few bruises; if not, it was too late to do anything about it now. I tried to whip that spotted horse up to something like a run.

I saw the rifleman then. He was standing as big as a barn on top of the highest rock on the hill, that battered old carbine looking like a toy in his enormous hands. I saw him, but even then I couldn't believe it. Not Vic Schuyler. Anybody else, all right, I would believe it. But not a big, easygoing guy like the foreman.

Even while I was trying to convince myself, I saw him put the carbine to his shoulder and take careful aim toward the dust cloud that Jane Albert's fallen horse had raised. I had to believe it then. I didn't know why. I wasn't sure that I wanted to know. For a moment I just felt sick.

I didn't have time to stop him, and I couldn't have stopped him anyway with a .45. It didn't make any difference, though, because Vic Schuyler never got that next shot away. Northern had already left his horse and was scrambling up the hill on his hands and knees. He put that fancy rifle to his shoulder and fired. The foreman jerked back, surprised. He almost lost his balance on the rock. Very carefully, he lowered himself to his knees and began climbing down from the rock. I could see the dark stain of blood spreading in the center of his dirty shirt.

We finally reached the hill, Jim Devers

and I. We left our horses and started up it, stumbling and clawing at rocks and weeds and anything we could get our hands on. And all the time, up on top, Northern and the foreman were blazing away at each other with their saddle guns.

'Stop it, I say!' the Sheriff kept yelling. 'Goddammit, stop that shooting!'

But the shooting went on and on until we had almost reached the top of the hill. Then suddenly it stopped. Somebody was dead. I didn't know who. I didn't even know why. But death was in the air.

The Sheriff and I lay behind a big rock at the top of the hill, panting after our climb. There was no sound except the wind, and now and then the dry flutter of a grasshopper.

'Northern,' I called.

No answer.

'Vic.'

Silence.

The Sheriff began swearing quietly, in that sober, serious way of his.

'Have you got any ideas?' I asked.

'Somebody better see about the girl.'

'I think we'd better see about this first.'

I fumbled around until I found a short stick. I put my hat on the stick and stuck it around the edge of our rock to see if somebody wanted to put another bullet hole in it. Nothing happened, so I stuck my head around and had a look.

'Well,' I said, 'we won't have to worry about Northern. He's dead.'

He was crumpled up behind another rock, kind of bent over with his arms spread out, as if he had just thrown six straight passes and was about to rake in the pot. The Sheriff and I slid from behind our rock and got behind Northern's.

'He got three in the chest,' Jim Devers said. 'He's dead, all right.'

I didn't touch him. I didn't look at him any more than I had to. I was tired of looking at dead people.

'Schuyler's probably dead, too,' the Sheriff said. 'They burnt enough ammunition up here.'

But I wasn't sure. And I was through

289

doing anything in Orlando County until I was sure. So I used the hat trick again. It worked this time. There was a crack of carbine and the slap of the bullet as it snatched a piece out of the brim.

We lay there wondering what we ought to do next. Maybe we could just wait and after a while the foreman would die — but we didn't know how bad he was hurt. A man like Vic Schuyler could take a lot of punishment. Anyway, I didn't like the idea much because there were still a lot of questions that I didn't know the answers to. I'd had a bad time in this place, and now I wanted to know why. It looked like Vic Schuyler was the only one left who could tell me.

'Look, Vic,' I called, 'it's no good this way. All we have to do is lay here and wait for the blood to run out of you. Why don't you throw that gun down and let us get you to a doctor?'

No answer. Just the wind and the grasshoppers.

'I don't know how you got mixed up in a thing like this,' I tried again, 'but we're willing to listen. We'll see that you get a fair trial. And there won't be any lynching — I'll give you my word on that if you'll come with us.'

I got an answer then. 'Go to hell, Reagan.'

It sounded like a man speaking through tightly clenched teeth.

'He still sounds pretty strong,' Jim Devers said. 'You see if you can work your way to the left; I'll back up and see if I can get behind him. Maybe we can box him in.'

It sounded like the best thing to do, so I started snaking around the other way, crawling from one rock to the other in the direction the foreman's voice had come from. I heard the Sheriff moving around the other way. We weren't making much of a secret out of it, but I was hoping that Schuyler would be too busy with his own troubles to bother about us.

He wasn't, though. I got behind a rock and he began wearing it down with that carbine of his. I checked my revolver and waited for the Sheriff to open up. It came finally, two big round crashes from Jim Devers' .45, and I knew that we had the foreman boxed.

I thought maybe he would give up then, but he didn't. He raised himself up from behind a rock and came staggering toward me, using his .45 now. At that moment he looked as big as a freight wagon and just as indestructible. He couldn't shoot worth a damn though, his gun arm was shattered, and that crazy, gimp-legged run of his didn't help much either. But he came on, and his face was a horrible thing, twisted and working in pain. Still, bullets seemed to have no effect on him.

The Sheriff was the one who finally got him, I think. The foreman's legs suddenly went to water and he crashed forward a few feet in front of me.

I took a deep, shuddering breath and holstered my revolver. I hoped that I would never have to use it again, on anything or anybody.

The Sheriff came over, his face a little grayer, his eyes a little more faded. He kneeled beside Vic Schuyler and turned him over. 'By God,' he said softly, 'he's still alive.' He shook his head as if he couldn't believe it. 'Still alive,' he said again.

But not for long. It was a matter of minutes now, or maybe seconds. He lay there looking at us, not with any kind of expression at all that I could see. There was nothing we could do.

The Sheriff stood up slowly. He holstered his gun and looked at his hands as if there was something wrong with them. 'Well,' he said at last, 'I'd better go see about the girl. You can wait here, Reagan.'

He walked away and I could hear him slipping and sliding down the slope of the hill, and after a few minutes I heard the pound of his horse's hoofs. Vic Schuyler still hadn't moved. Just his eyes, once in a while, would turn toward me.

I knelt down and straightened him out a little. His face began to work slightly. His mouth opened and closed a few times, as if he had forgotten just what it was for.

'What is it, Vic?' I said. 'Do you want to say something?'

It took some time, and the effort brought beads of sweat on his forehead, but finally he made it. 'You didn't — bring — a jug, did you?'

'I guess I let it slip my mind again,' I said. 'We'll pick one up, though, when we go by the ranch house.'

But I wasn't fooling him. He would never see the ranch house again and he knew it. 'Northern,' he said after a minute. 'What about — him?'

'Northern's dead,' I said.

He thought about it for a moment. It seemed to please him. He relaxed and was very quiet, and for a while I thought he had said all he was going to say.

But he wouldn't die. Not yet. He kept looking at me, and once in a while his mouth would work, as if he was a stage-struck kid about to say a speech, only he couldn't remember just how it started.

I said, 'You don't have to talk, Vic, if you don't want to. But if you feel like it,

I'll listen.'

A long moment went by and he seemed to be gathering strength for the effort. 'It all — started,' he began, 'the day — Kurt Basser rode — into town . . .' He talked for quite a while in fits and starts, before he died.

* * *

It was another hot day, the day we buried Kyle Northern and Vic Schuyler in the little two-by-four plot of ground just outside the New Orlando cemetery. Old man Palmer's nephew took care of the undertaking, and he did a pretty good job on them, considering. The usual number of curious ghouls came around to the funeral parlor for the viewing before the funeral, but practically nobody followed the hearse out to the burying ground for the final send-off. Just me and the Sheriff and George Albert, and a part-time Methodist preacher.

We gathered at the funeral parlor and helped Ralph Palmer — that was the nephew's name — get the coffins loaded into the black box wagon with the little diamond-shape windows in it, and then we waited until he whipped up his matched team of black horses, and we all fell in behind.

As we passed through Main Street the ghouls came out again to watch, but nobody was going to jeopardize his reputation by joining in on a rustler planting. Even Marcia Albert was among them. She was standing in the doorway of the dressmaker's shop as we went by. Her eyes were solemn, maybe even a little sad, but that was all. Poor Vic Schuyler.

I hadn't expected to see Jane Albert, but she was there, too, looking no worse for her experience the day before. When we got to the end of the block I saw her coming out of the doctor's office. She and the doctor had Ran Phillips between them and were helping him to a buggy that was pulled up next to the plankwalk. It turned out that Phillips wasn't hurt much, just a flesh wound in the thigh that would keep him out of the saddle for a while, but that was all. His eyes were bitter as we passed.

At first, I thought Jane Albert was going to face it out, but she broke down as we pulled abreast of them and began crying. *It's too late for tears now, Jane. Too late for regrets.* She was hanging onto the embarrassed Phillips, shaking with sobs. I tried to feel some pity for her. But pity wasn't in me that day.

So we crawled out of New Orlando and headed west on a lonesome dusty road, and after a while we could see the slanting tombstones of the town's respectable dead. The cemetery was boxed in with a low whitewashed rail fence, but that wasn't where we headed for. When we got to the gate we headed south along the fence until we came to a half a dozen unmarked mounds almost hidden in the weeds, and that was boot-hill. In death, a whitewashed fence separated the respectable and disrespectable, as nothing ever could in life.

Ralph Palmer brought his black horses to a halt before two fresh graves. Two grave diggers sat on the mounds of raw earth, watching silently, waiting for us to get the funeral over with so they could shovel the dirt back in and go home. We slid the coffins out of the hearse and placed them beside the graves; then we stood around awkwardly, hats in hand, waiting for the preacher to get started.

The preacher was nervous that day — maybe it was his first boot-hill funeral; he wasn't sure just how a thing like that ought to be brought off. But after a while he got started, and it didn't make any difference what he said, because I don't think any of us heard him.

George Albert took it harder than me or the Sheriff because he was naturally a trusting guy, and he was probably still seeing Vic Schuyler as a big, likable, loud-talking foreman whose only crime was taking a nip or two of rye whiskey while on the job. Albert's pale eyes were shocked and unable to understand what had happened. I didn't think he would understand, even if I told him, because that was the kind of man he was. In a way, I guess, he could understand Kyle Northern, because he had seen ambition in Northern before I had. But he didn't know the whole story. And he would never know it, if it was left up to me.

Finally it was over. We stood there listening and there was no sound but the rattle of dry grass in the wind, so we knew the preacher was finished.

George Albert put his hat on uncertainly, shaking his head. 'I don't know,' he said. 'I just don't see how they could have done it. I don't understand it, and I don't suppose I ever will.'

There didn't seem to be any answer to that, so the Sheriff and I said nothing. We went over to our horses and started back to town. When we reached the Sheriff's office, Albert said, 'Are you coming back out to the Box-A, Reagan? We'd be glad to have you if you want to come.'

'No, thank you,' I said. 'It looks like the job is finished now, so I'll be starting back toward the home office before long. I've got all my stuff with the Sheriff, so there's no use bothering you any more.'

Albert nodded absently. 'Yes, I didn't suppose you'd want to stay. I'll tell Marcia and Jane that you said good-bye.'

'Yes,' I said, 'do that.'

He hesitated before moving his horse out into the street again. He shook his head, puzzled. 'I just don't know,' he said again. 'It's going to take me a long time to get over this.' He held out a hand and we shook. 'I'm glad to have met you, Mr. Reagan, and I suppose that you did the job I asked you to do. But if I had known beforehand how it was going to end, I'm not sure that I would have called for you . . . I'm not sure at all.'

And with that he rode off. I saw him rein his horse in at the hitching rack in front of the dressmaker's shop, and I said, 'Sheriff, have you got any more of that sour mash?'

'You haven't told me everything, yet,' Jim Devers said, as he got tumblers out of his desk drawer and poured whiskey into them. 'Oh, I know generally what happened. Northern wanted to break the other ranchers, particularly Phillips, and grab off the water rights. And somehow he got Vic Schuyler to do the dirty work for him. That's the big type, but I can't read the little print in between.'

I sampled my drink. It was good whiskey, but the bottle was dangerously low. 'Well,' I started, 'as Vic Schuyler said, it all started the day Kurt Basser rode into town. Basser was a gambler. He had worked the gambling halls from Ellsworth on down, but the pay-off was a hitch he pulled in the Bull's Head Saloon in Abilene, and here's where the story gets complicated. Basser drifted into New Orlando and one of the first people he saw was a girl he used to know — or had seen, anyway — up in Abilene. She had been just a run-of-the-mill saloon girl then, fleecing the drovers, sponging drinks, picking up a nickel here and there any way she could. You can imagine his surprise when he finds out that the girl's name is now Marcia Albert.'

The Sheriff came half out of his chair. 'You're crazy!'

'Maybe,' I said, 'but that's the way it

was. I recognized her too, and almost got stabbed for it. I almost got my brains beat out that first night because Marcia had hired a pair of the Box-A's own riders to take care of me. But that didn't have anything to do with the rustling, except indirectly.

'Anyway, Basser recognized her, and when he started asking questions, Northern happened to be around. And it wasn't long before they had a deal cooked up between the two of them. Basser, I suppose, meant to squeeze some money out of Marcia with what he knew, but Northern had bigger ideas. He planned to use his new information as leverage and do some rustling by remote control. That was how he got Vic Schuyler in the thing, establishing the foreman as the boss rustler, taking all the risks, while Northern and Basser got all the money.'

The Sheriff said, 'I don't see how Schuyler ties into it all.'

'That's because you didn't know Vic very well,' I said. 'He was crazy about Marcia Albert. That's the only way I can explain it — he was crazy about her. And Northern knew it. So Northern put the proposition to him — if Schuyler didn't take over the rustling chores, spotting cattle for the raids, isolating herds, things like that, Northern threatened to start spreading the word about Marcia's past. Well, Schuyler couldn't take it, I guess, so he agreed.

'From there on it was pretty simple,' I said. 'Northern set Basser up in business with a little barbed-wire outfit down south, and pretty soon the gambler had the organization set up in Sand City. In his spare time he stirred up the small ranchers and drove the stolen herds over into New Mexico and sold them. That was how Basser came to have that money on him when I found him shot to death in the creek. He'd just come back from a selling trip. Northern' s money was in the money belt, but he had his own money in his boot where he thought it would be good and safe.'

'Money wasn't the only thing in the boot,' Jim Devers said. 'Money alone wouldn't have given the boss rustler away.'

I had another drink. 'I never got to know Kurt Basser,' I said, 'but he must have been a pretty shifty boy. Northern didn't trust him when it came to money, so when Basser went on a selling trip Northern made him get a receipt from the Indian agent, accounting for all the cows sold. The catch was that all those cows were supposed to belong to Northern, but he could never have raked up that many if he had been asked to account for them.

That was why Northern had to have that receipt, and the receipt was in Basser's boot, where the undertaker found it.'

'So Northern killed the undertaker and got the receipt,' Jim Devers said bitterly, 'while we were out chasing our tails.'

'And the girl — Jane Albert — saw him,' I said. 'That was the beginning of the end. Everything had gone pretty smooth until then. Of course, Northern had missed out on his bushwhacking try, the day I found Basser. But then I hadn't found anything anyway, so it didn't make any difference. And up until that time Vic Schuyler had been holding up his end of the bargain, one of his principal jobs being to get the posses lost in the badlands. That was why we couldn't find any trail after a raid. Schuyler would deliberately lose it — and that's easy to do in that country.

'But Schuyler wasn't happy about it. He wasn't the kind of man to stand for a lot of pushing around. He killed Basser himself. That night of the firecracker war. When we thought the rustlers had pulled out, Albert sent the foreman around to have a look. That was when he got Basser.'

I tried to remember back to that night and recall whether I had heard the shot. But that seemed a thousand years ago. I couldn't remember.

'He killed Basser, not knowing about the receipt and not giving a damn. Northern was next on his list, the next chance he got, and then Marcia Albert's past would be back where it belonged — in the past.

'But back to Jane Albert. It was Northern she was in love with, but there was something in her that was all twisted, and it made her keep baiting him about having no family. She kept showing him up against Ran Phillips and the Phillips family. God knows why. That's just the kind of woman she is. Or was. Maybe she has learned better now. But it's not going to bring Kyle Northern back to her.'

I got up and walked across the room, walked back again and poured another drink. There were just about two more drinks left.

'Well, finally Northern couldn't take it any longer. He figured he would break Phillips and run him out of New Orlando. Then he would break Albert too; anyway, whittle him down enough to make Jane Albert look up to Northern. That was when Kurt Basser rode into town, and Northern knew just how he was going to do it.

'That's about all,' I said, 'except a few

points that aren't very important now. That fight I had with Phillips in the saloon — that was Jane Albert again. She began to get scared after that funeral-parlor thing, so she must have told Phillips that I had been making some passes at her or something, probably hoping that Phillips would get mad enough to kill me. She was a cold-blooded little bitch, but she was still in love with Northern, and she wanted me out of the way before I got any smarter.

'It wasn't until near the end that she began to be afraid of what Northern might do to her because she knew too much. Actually, there was nothing to be afraid of, though, because Northern died trying to save her from Vic Schuyler. Vic knew about the funeral-parlor killing, of course, but he didn't know that the girl had seen it until yesterday when Northern made the mistake of telling him about it. That was what the argument was about when Phillips butted in and got shot. The foreman was afraid the thing would bust wide open and

Marcia's past would come leaking out, so he was in favor of killing the girl before she told anybody . . . Well, you know the rest of it. Vic was a little crazy, I guess, and maybe Northern, too. Women can do that to men sometimes.'

The Sheriff said nothing. He looked as if he had aged about ten years during the time I had been talking. At last he reached for the whiskey, emptied the stuff into the glasses and threw the bottle on the floor.

I don't know what the Sheriff drank to, but I had this one for Vic Schuyler. It wasn't rye, but it was pretty good whiskey, and I thought maybe he would appreciate it. I set the glass down and listened to New Orlando stirring uneasily in the hot afternoon. I tried not to think about the desert that I would be riding into before long.

★　★　★

It was almost sundown when I finally got Dusty from the old liveryman and got ready to put New Orlando behind me. The Sheriff was waiting in front of his office, and he came out to shake hands before I pulled out. 'I almost forgot,' he said. 'You've got that reward money coming. Where do you want me to send it when it comes in?'

I had to think for a minute to remember what he meant. Then I remembered old Huck and Kramer. 'When the money comes in,' I said, 'I want you to buy a tombstone — the biggest damn tombstone you can lay your hands on — and put it at the head of Vic Schuyler's grave. If you ask me why, I couldn't tell you. Except that I kind of liked him.'

Jim Devers shrugged slightly, not giving any argument. 'All right, I can do that, but that won't take all the money.'

'Then buy your wife a new dress. I never heard of an honest sheriff's wife that could dress the way she wanted to. And maybe some candy for the kids. And if you've got any money left after that, get drunk. Really roaring, down-in-the-gutter drunk, and try to forget for a little while that you're in the law business.'

And then I rode out of New Orlando. I looked back once and the Sheriff was standing in the middle of the dusty street, watching me. He lifted a hand in just a hint of a wave.

North of town we topped the little knoll and went past the cottonwood where I'd seen the two men hanging. I never did find out what happened to those boys. Probably they were down in boot-hill with Vic Schuyler and Kyle Northern, separated from the respectable dead by a white rail fence, waiting for the slow rot of time to smooth over the mistakes they had made.

I nudged that yellow horse of mine into a gallop and I didn't ease up until that knoll, and the cottonwood, and New Orlando, fell away on the other side of the sun-bloodied horizon. Then we settled down, going north.

Other titles in the
Linford Western Library:

VULTURE WINGS

Dirk Hawkman

Infamous low-lives, the Strong brothers will do anything for a quick buck — but this is going to be no ordinary kidnap. They are paid to abduct two young men, and don't ask too many questions when their paymaster gives them some unusual instructions. Then, as the boys' father races to rescue his sons, he realises that their snatching is linked to dark secrets from his old life as a bounty hunter.